High stilettos

Benjamin Benson Singh Bhamra

Published in 2017 by FeedARead.com Publishing

First Edition

A CIP catalogue record for this title is available from the British Library.

“I want to rip his nuts off.”

Hello and welcome back and this is my brand new show, we have got it all from guest actors to capital gaining gays. On the show today do not worry your secrets are safe with me and how did I come cross the last sentence I’ll be truthful I was watching shame on him really okay literally.
So how are you? “I’m fine. How the hell are you?”
“Is that your right hand or your left hand.?”
“In fact let’s forget about the hand shake”.
“Erma okay”.
So you do not mind me asking what is your ….
The guest I was talking to just up and left. His reply to the last question was that he was going for a smoke. I shouted after him, I’ll see you after the break good bye.

After the break.

Welcome back Are you good. That was good have you ever had one this was my first today. I know that I am a dirty little boy. And you love it and I like it however it is not for the kids so put it out before the producer tells your mum and then your mum tells my mum and so on. Any way lets go on all I want to do is talk about my dirty habits all day on.
The audience laugh.

Okay my next guest I asked how he was doing he replied pretty good it's cool.
After a few more question, my guest walked out all he said was that he was going for a cigarette and spoke as he was walking out. "Err yeah err no.
I could not figure out what he was saying.

High Stilettos

BENSON BENJAMIN SINGH BHAMRA

Welcome to my new talk show High Stilettos on this week's show we have a menu of guests including films stars and pop gurus. This is great, yes, it is, we also have some live music.
And we also have a movie mogul yes the biggest film star in Hollywood we also have some comedy from The three bad Meanies.
After the band had played I quickly closed the show and the re greeting and the greeting of half said thank you nice one and words of peace and all that stuff. I knew the streets so I would get down and party such is life. We will be back After the break. See you soon.
TV Commercial.

Welcome back ah is not life just wonderful I have been locked up yep sir but not as locked up as you would think all I had was some running gear and a pair of shades, but this pair of shades were special. They were a gift from my best friend and movie star. They were used in a couple of his movies they were funny extravagant and it's gay. All the lads would get huddled up the strum if you know what I mean. I always thought that rugby was for poofs and I might add so was football and probably American footballers as well as they huddle as well.
Go on take one.
Okay but do not say a word, can I have a light as well then.
Yes, you can. Indeed, you can.
Yeah that's nice what is it
It's a Cuban,

Is this the very cigar that you weld in your movies?
Yes, yes.
Now you have taken that you can get of my show.
Well as we near to the end of the show a break I have to say that smoking is really bad for your health as our actor proves to show us in his film.
He is the clip.

Okay who is next.
Whomever it is they are late. As the last group did not turn up I cut the show myself and introduced the bad meanies.
Now going back to smoking you have been a bad boy are you being bad and for your punishment I have sent myself to you yet again ….
I went on smoking in public places in full view I raised my hand s up like I was god or something along those lines and claimed he would suffer from now a dry mouth, and upset stomach, sickness and vomiting and the occasionally wet mouth and a big headache and to top it all off a bad sleep pattern and to top it all off drooling and over eating. Now be gone.

I'm off for a coffee.
He replied and walked off.

Hello and welcome to me to my show High Stilettoes on the programme for the night we have all the stars it will be a bit of a musical show this week and of course the tree meanies as well.
Good tonight's lesson is on masturbation. How well do you play?
What did I just say in fact I will just check that with the producer if I Just read that correctly err Masturbation, err yes that's correct. Well I have too admit I have not had the experience and I do not do that kind of thing. So hold on a second what's this oh its supper time, we will just take a short break while I eat this toast. See you after the break.
Well that was quick.
The producer had already queued me in as the wardrobe had was just dressing me up. What the hell is this. The word we're coming up on the camera quickly they read that the strange copse was my dad.
Dad is No.
I went into a state of shock. Dad it could not be you.
Sorry son but it is and I know what you are going to say, and I know you are not going to like what you going to hear as it is going to be a

little bit unsettling. But There was a pause there is a message from god for you.
I could not believe my eyes was I going insane, I Leant over the top of my desk, and tried to shunt him away as I was reading the script off the camera. Then I really lost it and started to if anybody else could see him, I continued Go away, get out, I was shouting your dead. Then the producer started questioning me as I hid in my arms on the desk. This cannot be happening.
No I replied and again no now get out.
He replied then have it your way.
At this point my understudy was about to step in and I just had time to tell the audience what was on next week's show.
It went something like this on next week's show and I was speaking really fast football, film stars and super models. The next day I was fired, a few weeks had passed and I was going to be a junior doctor. I had spoken about to friends and family they were not particularly interested. So I started to think about what Kinds of things I would be studying, I began with what's in the eye balls this was physiology I continued in the eye you have a pupil and retina the pupil can be enlarged and can also be small with vision. I have small pupils but in some cases they can be large, the actual eye consists of white flesh, the bigger part of the eye.
In the throat you have the Adams apple this helps you control talk and carry sound up to your mouth.
In the ear you have. I could not recall and went to the next subject, which was the toes as I said the toes were used for balance as well as grip for walking, with the toes you can use for balance, running.
From the heart are three main I paused for a second then continued there are three main pulses two in the wrist one on each wrist and one in the heart, you can also find the pulse in the leg around about the arci lies, around the top of the arci lies heel.
Going on the arms and in the arms, legs, toes, and fingers are joints these are surrounded by muscles properly ligaments to help bend and flex joints.
Also going back to the start of this note there on the right side or there about the kidney is the liver this helps digest food and waters, without a liver you would not be able to digest food.
Most of the human body is spiritual and in the forehead is there is a third eye. In the centre of the head and down through the body. The centre of the chest and down the middle of the body are chakras, in the

middle of the body the centre there are pressure points / also at each side right and left of your mind are pressure points these are called the temples. And under each ear there are pressure points too, all in all there are around one hundred to two hundred pressure points through the body.
In the back of the legs you have Araceli's tendon, calf muscle and ham string it is common in footballers that you can strain this muscle and it can be extremely painful. With the right healing it can be repaired. The knee and thigh there are also muscles on the thigh and around the knee. There are around four hundred ligaments in the human body. Food is digested by being taking into the mouth and chewed it is normal and to do this it takes around twenty or so chews. Then it has been made ready to swallow. It goes down into the tube, the oesophagus, into the stomach where it is digested. This may take an hour or so depending on how much you eat and how fast. The slower you eat the better.
In the stomach there are acids, they breakdown the food for indigestion.
In the eyes they are filled with brain fluids and the water known as tears, when you get upset it is common that you would cry. This realises the emotions of happiness and sadness. They can be both physically and emotionally draining. If you cry to much you could cause yourself harm. In the body there are also lungs. With these we would not be able to breath. What would happen if we did not have lungs, I guess that all the air would go to our stomachs. It is possible to breath threw our lungs. In the lower part of the body we have the pelvis attached to this we have the penis and in the woman the virginals. Going back to the eyes the eyes are attached by veins and the veins go to the head which go to the brain. At the end of your arms you have the wrists and you can use them to maunder your hands you can use your hands to pick items up, draw, punch, drop, and clench objects and so on. In the mouth you have a tongue the tongue is used for tasting and the nose is used for smelling, although the nose is a passage for air it can be filled with mucus and germs and the throat can be cleared when the symptoms occur. I have a question. How many times does the average human sniff per day? and would you use a tissue for this. Sounds stupid doe it not.
The blood cells consist of water and blood cells which are white and red. The neck there are six bones. What makes up the human body. Well in the human body you have an elbow and a fore arm. The arm

also has a bicep which are both muscles the lower back of the legs you have calf muscles. In the back of the foot you have a heel the muscle is called the Achilles if this snaps you would be unable to walk.
Going on to diseases there are many types such as cancer, aids /HIV and which all lead to death. There are many types of cancers there are over seventy types of cancers that the human body can suffer from or can affect the human body. In the world today the most common effect of cancer is caused by smoking or over exposure to the sun, heat. You can also die of throat cancer although you can have your throat replaced. The second is lung cancer again you can have a lung transplant. There are also other diseases such as kidney failure. Again these parts can be replaced.

Bowl infection, heart failure, you can have a transplant although it is more than likely that the heart that you have will come from a pig rather than the human body.
There are other diseases that the human body can catch sicknesses and colds such as the influenza, chest colds and headaches. There are such things as skin disorders such as exam, blisters and cold sores. These so called cold sores can exist in the mouth. That's why it is important to keep the mouth clean. Abscess in the mouth can be caused by over brushing. You can use salt, a mouth gel such as sialon or bonjela to clean the mouth.
Finger and thumbs the thumb is quite important too without thumbs you will not be able to hold objects and you will not be able to pick objects up. The hand is the only part of the human body they cannot be replaced or replicated synthetically
The veins in the arm lead to and through the hand reaching the very end (the finger tips) of the hand.
There are also pressure points in between the thumb and the fore finger and they are for healing.
In our eyes lids which shields us from the light and dust particles that are in the air. At night when we sleep they are closed to help us sleep.
On your eyes you have eye lash these are there to protect your eyes and keep them clean.
You can open and close your mouth this is controlled by muscles in the jaw and sensors in brain.
At the end of our arms we have hands these are used for holding things such as objects for instance glasses for a drink or even more so a pot

for cooking and more importantly making things and doing things in general.

In your hand at the middle you have five knuckles these exists in both hands, at the bottom of your feet you have the sole these are what we walk upon. In the foot you have an ankle and a heel and toes and balls. Without these you would not be able to balance at the sides of the head you have ears these also help you to balance.

Growth and nutrition, calcium is needed to control bon e growth mostly when you were a child it is also needed to help the growth of teeth we use tooth paste to do this it will clean the enamel. Keeping the mouth clean reduces the chance of disease.

We have hair on our bodies to keep us clean and in some cases to protect us. We have around the pelvis area, on our heads, our face, legs and arms, chest and back. Woman can also grow hair but it is most that they are likely to shave it away.

In the back is a large bone called the vertebrae this consists of lots of bones connected together at the bottom of this there is a lower bone which is used for balance.

Below this you have your bottom this is a muscle it is strong and is used to sit, walk, run. The rump is one of the most powerful of the human bodies accessories close to the brain and heart.

On the end of the metatarsal there are nails these are used to protect our fingers.

The knowledge was beginning to flow every word, letter and sentences sent a racing beat of excitement to my mind. The feeling of the power of knowledge had blown me away I could not believe the knowledge that I was gaining, it was incredible.

On the day I could not do it I could not bring myself to do it. I gad dreams of the day that my wife would die. The feeling was incredible my whole body was trembling with the thought. All I could see when I closed my eyes was her was she a spiritual woman, she was a doctor. It was big business at the time and the business was good. She was good but she had to go, for a lady she was quite talented. What she did not know was that she was alone. She laid there asleep as I watched her. It was the right time I could feel it, I closed my eyes once more I could clearly see her. I was not a happy person as such I rubbed my eyes but the images did not change. The feeling of darkness had arrived in to my soul. I counted to ten each time taking a step closer to her bed. She was laid there on top of the duvet which was on top of the bed. She was semi -naked, I leant down over her I could feel her breathing. I was not sure at the time how I was going to do it. I suppose to myself I could have been anybody but this was not me. I was a talk show host, mega rich, mega famous how could I get caught, I could not. I continued to look at her body in my eyes she was still quite beautiful looking. But I had had enough I was board waiting it was time. How was I going to kill her? I guess the old fashion way was too odious, I pulled a pair of gloves out of my pocket. I had to think very cleverly I could not leave any prints anywhere. I slipped off my shoes and approached her she was fast asleep she must have had a hard day at work. I took another step forwards toward her. It was now just a matter of time. We had good times for a few years anyway when we first met I thought she was an incredible woman she was nice and fit. But there was something wrong it was she had become cold, she would not speak to me, days of silence, and a bad attitude. The party's that we had I think she just grew ungrateful. This was making me feel sad just thinking of her. We had flown around the world together. I had fallen out of love with her, she had become like a stone and I wanted to throw that stone as far as I could away from myself. In a way she had broken my heart. As I took another step closer the blood was blistering through my veins flowing and in was hot. For some reason I forgot what I was doing as my attention turned towards my bedroom curtains I pulled up a chair and waited I could see my cat and it looked like he had made a kill he was dragging something I think he caught mouse. Going back to the conversation of how was I going attempt the murder of the wife I could just blow her head off although that would be a bit noisy I suppose as she is always in bed I could smother her with her pillows. She was too strong for that I was only a small and not particularly strong. I have a knife maybe no I think it would be too messy I could just cut her wrists and make it look like suicide. I could poison her that thought stayed with me. I needed time to calculate this thought

I considered myself as one of the good guys I never made any trouble and when trouble come s looking for me I would normally disappear. Nobody really new me out side of the world of TV. I had loved my job. I closed my eyes for a moment so I could think. For some reason I was feeling guilty for the planning of the murder of my wife. When I was alone it already felt like she was dead anyway so it did not make any difference. It was not like me to smoke more than two cigarettes in a day so I thought I would have another. I Pulled the smoke casually out of its packet and pushed it into my mouth then lit it up the smooth taste was giving my soul a cool sensation as I breathed it into myself. As I did this I was looking up at the sky it was going to rain the sky's clouds racing past each other and the light of the day rapidly changing from sky blue too dark grey. I stood there outside and waited for the rain. A few more moments for the clouds too hind the sun and it was set a storm had begun. I walked back in to my house making my way to the kitchen, where the windows were dirty blinding me from the storm and its electrical night mare the lightening.

As I was in the kitchen I made the opportunity to cook. As it was getting darker through the storm I turned on the lights making a clicking sound it was weird the sound of the light switch seemed to echo click, click, click. I threw something on the stove together quickly not that I was in a rush that was the way I cooked. By the time it was ready I had lost my appetite, I sat at the dining room table staring at the plate of food. It was not that the food was badly cooked I just could not bring myself to eat it. I pushed the plate of food away from me leaving enough room to put my arms on the table and buried my head into my arms and closed my eyes.

I was no longer in love with myself or my wife which was becoming more and more obvious. The storm had finished and the rain was drying up. I had slept most of the day on my dining table. I was thinking about going to work but the thought of being in the same room as wife just put me off even more.

I had a plan I was going to kill my wife, I went through it over and over, again until it was perfect or I until I thought it was. The timing had to be perfect dinner at seven deaths by eight. I went upstairs to find my past port as I had planned to leave afterward the deed was done. I looked at the past port it was in date. I would drive straight to the airport. I was sure that my alibi was good enough to have myself escape. I did not need her money as I had plenty of my own. That meant that I did not have to mess around with credit cards and banks which would cost me time and could leave evidence.

All of a sudden my thoughts came to a holt and there was a calm ness about myself. I could feel it around me and in the house, then the tears came they flooded my eyes I was slowly beginning to realise how sorry I was and properly be but I shook it off. In the house there was nothing to do everything was done it was extremely tidy and I was glad that it was so. It was a reasonable size and I was slowly falling out of love with it, that's the wife fault. The celling was high and it had Oaked beams. There were chandlers in most rooms on the celling. I had the whole house fitted with carpets and to my advantage I had a study filled with books on anatomy and physiology. The best part of my home was the furniture the books on medicine.

I waited in the bathroom for a few minutes I was scared. Later on in the day I went to approach her to see if she had calmed down. After another fight I presumed that She was busy choosing her dinner friends but I could not find her anywhere. I presumed as she was not around that she had gone to work. It was a little bit disappointing every time I had my chance to out my grasps upon her she manages to get out of the situation.

I felt kind of hot, I looked down upon myself I was sweating I touched my fore head I was perspiring.

I looked under my arms for the first time in about ten years there was sweat. I could not recall the last time I perspired I took the shirt off and went into the bedroom for a clean shirt and changed it for a fresh one. In about fifteen minutes it had happened again. I thought for a minute it was probably pressure of the thought of murdering my wife. For the rest of the day I was in the kitchen, cooking it was something that I did when I had the time and it was something I did because I was good at it. I was making a curry. I found it therapeutic, All the chopping and stirring. I could not wait for the dinner party. I guess cooking for that lot would be a doddle.

As I was cooking you know simmering the food I opened up another packet of cigarettes and lit one the smooth sensation hit my throat and blowing out smoke made me feel a lot calmer, when I was finished smoking I stubbed the butt out on the side of the chopping board the smell of the smoke sang to my brain as I stood their sucking in the contaminated air it was not good for you I opened the window, trying to suck in the air as I with the frying pan which was over filled with food. As I calmed the pan down. As I did not really smoke a lot maybe just on the occasion. I was looking out of the window thinking that it was peaceful. The trees blowing in the wind sending and the shadows of the plant life shadows in the sun. The reflection of myself I bowed myself down only to look up at a flock of birds flying away from me. I went to the door to open it to let in some fresh air. I was sure that I was burning up. I was standing up in the kitchen watching my rice boil slowly the weather changed again within one minute it went from reasonable good to total rain. I stood there watching it once it had stopped a long hard grey mist occurred and blocked the trees, bushes and road it was kind of spooky. It reminded me of something that you would see in a film.
I looked up again at the sky the clouds had gathered their momentum again it looked like it was going to rain again, and it did as always it started with the clouds and the sky changing. The colours were incredible from white skies to a deep grey, then the wind sped up the skies were pushing the clouds around faster and faster, then the rain storm, then on top of that the thunder. Quickly twisting and turning, it was loud then the storm rain, just before the lightening then nothing. I decided to brave the storm weather and headed out side.
I was in darkness it was it was like a warning saying stay indoors but I did the opposite I stayed outside lightly covered by a small shelter I stood and that's where I watched the thunder storm it was only there for a few minutes it seemed like a life time.

She walked up to me, she had that look in her eyes like me and her she was up for it you know sex, she put one hand on my cheek I was feeling hot, my pulse was racing. I thought a last that I was going to get sex if you know what I mean. But nothing she turned and walked the other way. I stunned by her actions what asked her as I called out to her what do you want, don't you want me. She turned around and walked back towards me I thought that she was going to kiss me and everything was in place if you know what you mean. I grabbed her holding her tightly and cried out well it was more of a shout. "What". She slapped me around the face and pushed me into the corner of the room. Is that fore play I asked myself then she hit me again I must have been out of mind to except it, but I did and the way she put her hand on my face I will never forget it.

Then we met again this time I was in my car and without a glance, she did not even okay me. I pulled up and got out. I asked her if we could take a walk. For the first time I had a decision and it was the first time that I was actually scared. I told myself something different just so I could walk with her. Once I had settled down I was like I'm there. Her sexy dress was beginning to pull me again it had sex all over it and to top it off she was under the influence of alcohol. I had a couple of questions that I wanted to ask her so I continued I began with how much have you had to drink? The reply was I have had a bottle and a bit, and yes I am drunk to answer the question. She had cornered me again this time she pushed her hand out upon my chest. Pushing me backwards and forcing me to grab her hands it was seductive. Come in she replied I chose to ignore her last comment as it was my house. I Smiled just the thought of what she wanted and what she thought but she never knew that what she wanted was going to happen.
I was having a quiet afternoon and all I wanted was to go home and get into a hot bath. As I drove into my drive I was glad I was home. With the engine still on I looked up my wife was just behind me. She pulled up just behind me so I could not get my car into the right parking space. I beeped her Couple of times she opened her window slowly putting the cars gear in order. She just looked at me then slowly put her window up. I could tell that she was ignoring on purpose, I knew by the expression on her face. I knew she knew that I knew as well. That was it I started to sweat, she really had upset me. I got out of the car she did not think to think that I needed the space. Just as I

was approaching the mansion, she caught up with me quickly I could see that she was not in a good mood. Also I could see more clearly that she did not want see me. But she knew and I knew that It I wanted her to move her car. She was still quite polite which amounted for something I guess but on this occasion I wanted to ring her bloody neck. I got back into the car sweating and in rage and anger. When she finally came outside she was simply dressed, which was quite sexy, her long brown hair running down her back. She got into her car and reversed it past my car and back into her normal parking space. Again she was not particularly polite. She got out of the car and went back into the house.

Again I had to laugh there was something weird going on in my life I was thinking about the things that were going on in my life, it was probably a normal thought of everyday life.

I did not know whether I needed a drink, at this time as I was walking through the hospital, to the car park to get to my car. I had found it and I was standing by the door the front door.
I looked for my keys and found them in the inside of my jacket pocket. I opened the door which was cold to touch and seemed heavy and got in.
The clouds were gathering and it looked to me that there was another storm brewing. I sat inside my car looking at the weather Still thinking that there would be a storm.

It was quite a lonely place like darkness in darkness.

CHAPTER 2
Who laughs last

It was not until after I had I finished the drinks and I was half drunk and all I could do was laugh. And laughing at the incident one after the other. Almost straight away. I walked back to shop when two pedestrians ran past with what looked like a till. One of them ran into me knocking me to the floor smashing the till open there was money everywhere. I was too drunk to be able to grab some as the thief quickly grabbed what he could then continue to run. They left me on the floor all I could see was concrete.

I was laying on the hard concrete floor, it was brittle the lights from the street lamps shone down upon me blinding my eyes for a few seconds as I picked myself up of the hard floor
I was speaking to the shop keeper who was slowly behind me he was kind enough to ask if I was okay.
And helped me to my feet.
I walked the shop keeper back to the shop I asked him if it was okay to buy a beer the answer was obvious NO.
Then he changed his mind I was cool with that he asked my name and what I was doing following the patience. I said nothing then I said just past me a beer. Then he asked me if I was a doctor. I just looked at him and he just looked at me. I had just finished work and all I wanted was a pint. The police turned up.
Properly for the old man as he had just had his till nicked. I was keeping my cool the police basically asked me the same question as the shop keeper and I was trying to explain that it had nothing to do with me all the police said as from what I had told them I was now a witness. I refused to talk to them and in was trying to explain that I was a doctor and all I was on a brake. I was in deep shit. For some reason they seemed to be focused on me rather than being focused on the shop keeper. I walking out as I did I shouting and singing that there was no crime in shopping. I stood in the ally way drinking what was left of the beer. I could not help but smile thinking about the teenagers. I could only imagine what they would do next.
I sat down in the ally way I thought about what had just happened again so I got in between the two patience they were both dressed in hoods matching hoods, jeans and scruffy trainers one of them was female. The girl seemed to shuffling around a lot I think that she was pretending to look for some money. And looked distressed I was going to help but I had already had my hands full with a pack of beers. My money was good and as I was the next customer I thought that I would pay for her. I just thought I should give her a tenner I took the ten pound out of my wallet and payed the shop assistant and told him to get hers too.
Her reply was what are you doing. THAT'S a good question I thought I understood that she had a slight problem with her manners in a nice way of course.
I would like to pay for that, that upset her even more she said no grabbing her bag I have got my own money that's when I snapped look I said I am a doctor. I have my identification I said slowly

calming down. I stuck my hand into my pocket but there was nothing. I tried again asking her to be patience again. But again nothing. Shit I thought that I had another note. Time was getting on after weighing up the kid's behaviour I guess you could call it legit. I left the shop promptly After I had finished drinking in the ally way I made my way back to the hospital. I had decided that I was going to live it up a bit you know what I mean get smashed.
I had not seen my wife all day I guess she was busy anyway, after I had a long think about the wife I decided to get even more drunk I went back to the off licence. I had always had a problem with drink. It was not like I would drink heavy. Or that I could not handle It is not like I cannot control my habits It was not like I did not know I enjoy it but when there is nothing else that's where the pain is.
I walked to the shop again I knew where it was and I was lucky that knew the way back as I was drunk. As a doctor you tend to notice everything. As I walked back to the hospital, I spent a lot of the time working with mental health patience, they were taken out every two hours and waited for the opportunity to join them as they all walked out I snuck in. nobody noticed me and I had done this a couple time before. I think it was funny that nobody actually noticed leaving me to believe that nobody really cared.
I was six paces behind the crew it was crazy, exciting., sorrowful and loving all at the same time watching and listening.

It was late in the afternoon about one thirty I was not feeling so good as for last night. I was not feeling tired but I could have closed my eyes but I was worried about this, I was worried about what I was going to see. All the dreams and all the visions it was like I was dying I believed that I had no memories and I had lost the will to have a consciousness. All the time that I was studying It was like I was dead, but I knew that I was still alive. I also knew that I had a soul somewhere inside of me.
Or maybe I did not have a soul. Maybe it was just coincidence. I was just trying to piece it together it was all getting to much. I felt the way I did because I did, and I felt deeply for my wife. I had chosen to keep the truth about our relationship aside for now. I felt the temperature drop it was cold. I did not know why I was feeling this way I was un sure it was a different feeling for me.
As I worked my way up to the tenth patience I was going out of my mind, it was racing with excitement. It was a good environment to be

in. I knew that I was in love with the place. I did not make one mistake all day. Everything was going well considering that I was a junior doctor and it was my first day back for a few months.
I would have thought that the boss would have made an appearance just to give me a blocking.
But nothing, it was time for a break, I had just one more patience to see. I did not notice at first That's when it happened. At first it took me by surprise a lot. I was just about to take my stethoscope off when I noticed the shadow of a figure walk by me. He came across as clumsy where was he going I asked the question to myself as I thought that I was the only one that saw him.
He was walking slowly at first but as I followed him he seemed to pick up the pace. The hospital was busy and I thought I had lost him but I caught him in my eye again, a small chase had occurred. I Pushed my way through the crowds of people all waiting for the doctor. He was quick he was too quick for me he was gone. I made my way back to my office. The strange man had disappeared.
I walked back to my office there was some old lady kicking off that was half of my worries. Feeling disappointed that I never caught the mysterious man. It rattled my brain who could it have been. Although taking my mind back way back in to the past he seemed familiar

I was dreaming it felt different being away for so long. My mind was racing in excitement I was about to receive the first job of the evening. I closed my eyes and took a deep breath. I was at work.
Give me the chart That was the first thing I asked for it to be handed to me. I read it out loud quickly.
It was not hard it was just in medical terms. Then silence I was lost it was likely I had fainted except I was wide a weak. I was reading the chart it was all out of order I had to put it back into English I shouted who wrote this and took another look at it. I knew latten and I managed to translate with a little bit of luck someone was trying to test me, then my mind went blank due to the confusion. The pressure in my eyes was building. I began to become light headed. Then silence I had lost my mind again. A voice called out two or three times Then I snapped out of it I was being woken up the hard way.
I hated to go outside so I told my team that I needed some fresh air. I made my way out and found a space just inside of a door way, IT was raining I was getting wetter and wetter I stood there for ages or it seemed that way. I walked to my car which was parked near and when

I got there I opened the boot I had a couple of pairs of jeans in there the reason for this is that in my line of work there is always someone being sick down you. I was sober enough to change my clothes. I caught my reflection in the door of my car. It was like a long stare into darkness. I pulled up my hood over my head. Drying my hands to get the wet off them. Then slipping them into my pockets I walked as back fresh a baby. Walking through the main doors like I cool or something shutting the doors behind myself. I was trying to get my head around my problems and around my situation. Everything that I had discussed was staring me right back in the face. I walk back to A E. I wiped the rain drops of my face with a shimmy leather which I am still trying to work out why. I was entering the AE it was busy. Some of my work mates in they welcomed me back there were chants of appreciation such as Your good and here's mister cool. The night went on it was getting busier and busier when I finally got out of the place and got home.

The wife was in the building also still going on pretending about how good I was but she was lying if you took a good look you would properly see you could see the look on her face that she was jealous. When all the excitement was over she had disappeared I closed my eyes I was half listening to her and half listening to the shower that she was in. I could see that it was nice and hot. She twisted around the water as the water fell upon her. She was in and out in about forty minutes I could hear her speak out about how good that it was. She said something that it was so good that she could wash her woes away. I thought that I should have been in there with her. I was only there in my mind.

By the time she had finished I was no longer worried. I met her on the way out we had switched places for a moment she had gone upstairs and I had gone into the shower. After about half an hour I got out of the shower and got dry. I had bared myself slowly and walked back into the bedroom. She was laying on the bed half down it on her side with the bedding half down herself. She looked quite stunning still after everything that we had been through. She thought that I was to die for but it was going to be the other way around. I closed my eyes she was pretty good giving me the cold shoulder well I was not particularly bothered at this time. A beer and cigarette was just as good. She was asleep and I was half awake sitting upright in our bed. I was half way through a cigarette. When she stared to talk in her sleep. You would not believe what I had heard the words do it again. Came out of her mind, I was hoping that it was me she was dreaming about. There was a couple more sentences which came out but I could not make her say them again. I felt like pushing her off the bed. Then half asleep she through her arms upon me I presumed that she was still asleep. And started to kiss me my eyes filled with tears. I closed my eyes she was good I thought this time it was all good she asked me to do it again. She was an animal she leapt on top of me but with an instant I had to push her off. She made me say that I was not ready. She was all for it.

If she did this in her unconsciousness I could not imagine what she did at work, when she was there.

Her dreams continued she was talking about all crazy sexy things everything kind of slipped out. Her words had begun to worry me. She was clearly out of her mind. She turned over again in my direction and I just pushed her off. I got off the bed and walked to the bathroom semi naked.

Turned on the shower and got in it, the water was cooling my mind in fact it was totally relaxing.

I closed my eyes pushing the water over and over myself. The wife was in the bedroom still, I closed my eyes half listening to her. It was nice I twisted around in the water as it fell upon me. I bathed for a round an hour it felt so good washing my thoughts and woes away. By time I had finished I was completely relaxed, I thought of nothing. I asked her if she wanted to take a shower she replied later. I dried myself up and bared myself. As I was looking around the bedroom for a t-Shirt I found my wife lying face down and half on her side with the bedding half slid down her. It was quite a frill. I was looking forwards to the dinner party I did not look at her for long as I was ready to go back to work I of got the feeling of love back. All the thoughts of killing her had escaped my mind and as I had a clear mind I was thinking clearly again. Before I left I walked to her dressing table, where her clothes were. They were dirty so I got some clean clothes out of the closet for her. It was getting late and I had to be at work. I closed my bedroom curtains to shut out the rest of the light. I grabbed a belt from my chest of draws. I continued to watch her in her sleep. So perfect and quaint I had a weapon a killing weapon I leant over her and whispered her name but nothing not a sound. I could strangle her, she would not feel a thing I told her, I took my trouser belt of holding with my hands at either end twisted in both hands pulling it tight. I was close to the edge and so was she. I looked at her and I looked real hard. I could not do it; it was the wrong time I pulled my self together quickly.

As I put the belt back on walking out the bedroom. Slamming the bedroom door to wake her on purposely. I stood by the door waiting for her reaction she looked up lent over and then back before falling out of the bed. I closed the door quietly and leaving her on the floor and then left of work.

I got down stairs quickly a bit too fast I had a sick feeling inside of me for a while. I closed my eyes for a moment, I got the car keys out hesitating and dropping them on to the floor I picked them up in a hurry I pushed the car key into the door opened it and got in. It was clean right through as usual it had escaped my mind for the moment the only reasonable answer was that the Valier got the wrong car and cleaned mine instead of the wife's easy mistake I thought as I was one for saying that I do not make mistakes. I pushed the stereo radio on and put the keys into the ignition and set it up for a drive, the engine roared I rolled her out and drove out of the drive way. My mind was racing I was thinking about the sex we had just had it she was good I thought there was no doubt. But it was not love and that is what hurts, it was hate. I only did to satisfy myself and my ego and I knew that she thought the same. I took a smoke from the filled packet and lit it up. Then out of nowhere a police car appeared in the rear window mirror I was not sure if he was going to pull me over. I looked down at the dash board checking everything and everything was in order only that I was just over the speed limit. I did not think that they would pull me over for that. The police car did not seem to be to bothered as I said. I thought that they were going to nick me for speeding they had their lights on lucky they just drove past me. I thought that I was quite lucky considering the kind of things that I was thinking. I pulled up over in a layby. I closed my eyes and thanked god not that I was a fan of god. But it was funny he was there when I needed him and always as I was heading for trouble. In saying that it can always work both ways as you will see. I pushed the accelerator down I was speeding again when I past them on the opposite side of the road the police were pulling some guy over I shot pass them clearly getting their attention. When they caught up with me I had my license ready as they approach my window before the policeman even got to the car I knew exactly what I was going to say, I wound down the window electronically. He questioned me I said that I was on the way to the hospital and showed him my ID. I was a doctor he checked my ID again for a few minutes passing it to his partner for night. I tried to explain to him that I was in a rush as I had to be in surgery. He past the ID back with a ticket. They waited for me to go but I did not because at that point I was parked up at the edge of a ravine. The idea just popped into my head I could just fake my own death the police were long gone which gave me the opportunity to take a look around although that it was not that far down it could work however there would be nobody there to witness it. I thought about it more carefully more and more ideas racing through my mind I Could leave the car down there I could throw away my coat, but I did not want to leave any evidence

I really thought hard to make it work eventually my idea came to the end. About a minute or two in to the drive to the hospital I drove passed the police again I was going about a hundred and a bit more they pulled me up fast. I could not be bothered to start a chase even before they had pulled up me up I was pulled up in the lane by the edge of the road. I knew the outcome a speeding ticket and probably a fine. The officer approached the car for the second time for the night. I looked at the officers approaching. I turned off the engine and opened the window.

Hello officer.

Do you know.

I interrupted him in an instance, I know that I was speeding. The conversation went on I was trying to keep it as brief as possible and then the police man asked me to step outside of the car.

He was going to breathalyse me I had no choice but to accept. He then asked me to get out of the car and walk in a straight line. Then he asked why I was speeding

It was only now that I thought of what it must feel like being killed. Waiting up half dead and struggling to do things, simple things like dressing or making a cup of coffee. Or even just to get yourself washed. Once I thought being dead would lead to the next life but it was more than that.

I think that maybe in some religions there is just the thought of enlightenment, not that I am looking forward to coming back as a snake or a bird or even one of the big five even more so I could come

back as myself. I did not know all the answers. Being a doctor is not being like god. I mean yes it feels like god when you save somebody it's life one day is good the other days may be bad. But was a daily thing you can understand that's just the way it is.
I had half a smile on my face I could not believe it myself I just gave myself a grilling I thrashed my own mind without my wife doing for me I guess I was insane.
There was a tear in my I squinted to remove it I was not upset I was happy always and honest I really was really happy I was telling myself that everything was going to be fine I was climbing out of the ravine, pushing the trees branches aside when I got to the top it was muddy and I had to be careful not to slip. When I got to the top I realised that my foot prints were there and it took me a few more minutes to decide if I should go back down there to cover my tracks I made my way down there again this time covering my tracks pulling the leaves of the trees and laying them down over the foot prints I hoped it would be enough. I climbed back to the top and got into my car. And I took a big sigh with it.
So throwing myself down big hill was a no no. Even if I did fake my own death there would be question and where was my body surely there would be someone who would ask. I tried to think.
I was thinking so hard I began to sweat, a round an hour later the thought of the evening events
Had aspired back into the death of my wife I begun to calmly put the thoughts down and calm down and concentrate on the journey to the hospital, I was just about to make it on time which was unusual for me as I was always late and when I was ready to use the only excuse there was an accident or it was the traffic or I had forgotten my lunch and had to go back home. As I pulled into the car park as I was I was nudged from behind. I leaped out of the car shouting this is a porches' my darling my darling.
The driver who was behind was apologetic she replied that she was sorry and gave me her insurance details I knew that she was going to start clicking on to me. She fiddled with her papers like a nervous rack I told her to move it as I was already late now that only caused her more distress. then as she got back into her verse. I walked around the back of the car checking out the damage it was minor a small dent and a tiny scratch.
The lady looked quite rich thinking about it and the thought of smashing the dent in bigger had come to mind as she did not examine

the dent she would not know, and I could make a quick buck not that I needed the money but it was something to do. She did not resemble any one important I could remember her clearly she was touching her brow and waving her hair as to say oh my what have I done and clicking on at the same time. I knew that she was trying to keep me sweet.

CHAPTER 3
Moving to fast

The rest of the evening moved on slowly as time seemed to move fast although it went reasonable well. The first patience that I had a broken leg the second had burns the third had a problem with his age he was a bad mouthed bickering fool. I knew it had something to do with his age and all I wanted him to do was to shut hell up. I could have told him myself but it was part of my job to be polite. But no one said anything about bribes so I found a young person put twenty quid in her hands and told her what to do. She went over to the man and started to scream right next to the man there was silence throughout. I smiled at her she smiled back and the old man had shut himself up. I signalled her to go and she did. But that did not work The old man then started on about all kinds of things first it was his arm then within about five minutes it was his feet this was on going then it was his head. This time I lost my temper I grabbed him this time I told him to shut the hell up there are people about you that are just as unwell as you, that's when he shouted my ear. This time I raised my voice turning the manager towards me I quickly came up with a diagnoses ere r I hesitated nurse this man needs some medication I quickly wrote it out on paper and gave it to the nurse. The old man finally shut up.
I could not get the old man of my mind and being old was his excuse. The nurse gave him the injection. Thank god for that I thought that it was going to go on forever like all night. The rest of the patience began to clap and large cheers were heard. By the time I was finished it was late. I strolled to the car park. Where I thought the porches was well I thought it was. I always, always parked in my space it had my name on it but the car was not there. I checked everywhere my first thought that it had been stolen I had the keys right in front of me but it made no difference the car was gone.

I kind of thought it was funny I was not going to let it upset me. You know what they say what goes around comes around. I had no choice I was not comfortable talking to the police so what could I do I suppose I could do what every teenager dreams of doing and steal a car. I was looking around for a car but I could not find one. In the end I just tried to thumb myself a lift home, but that did not work I looked around for a brick it was the ultimate weapon if you wanted to break into a car along with the crow bar and bolt croppers. But I did not think that I would find anything like that around here maybe in a boot of a car but it was not that I needed as I already had a brick, I walked up to the biggest jeep I could find and threw the brick within seconds two or maybe three others car alarms went off in either direction I legged it back to my car space.

I sat down in sorrow crossed legged on the cold concrete floor the wind blowing my hair and the cold on my face. I decided to take the bus home.

I had to take a sip of wine at the table it was sombre and dark to my eyes but in reality it was light.

I sighed with the refreshing pleasures and gave a large burp, my soul was lit up I took another mouth full. The dining table was adequate and some picture on either side of it of my family. I did not like discussing my family with other people, friend s or not it was very personal for me. But on this occasion I was sucking the history in if you know what I mean I took another mouthful of the wine.

I was reasonably well off now I had a rich family and everything was laid on a plate for me even medical school. As a teenager I would collect insects and other things it became a fascination.

The thought of the day was to murder my wife. I have always said it she was a real bitch. In the end there was nothing I liked about her and if her snootiness was not enough. We met when we were at college then again at medical school we spent the whole time together. Well I would not be going through this if it was not for her. I Was drunk and I did not know how much I had drunk that night but I was a state in the morning, there was beer and wine bottles everywhere I had that dream again the one where I would be strangling my wife to death, every time I have this nightmare I wake up outside or climb out of the bathroom window. without my keys to get back in then it takes me two hours to get the wife up but lucky I was prepared I had hid my spare keys under a brick in the garden hoping that I would remember them

ion this occasion I had woken up outside and I had forgotten about the keys so I threw the brick though the window to wake the wife up and then saw the keys. She came down stairs in a really bad mood. She did not have to say anything I knew. That early morning, I felt so scared of her I finished the rest of my sleep on the sofa. I did not tell anybody about my dreams not even my wife she believed that I was just sleep walking and my wife gave me written consent to take her to court if she talks.
Mind you looking at the window after I awoke the next morning gave me the idea of I could always push her out of the window and use the psychotic episode as the alibi. Come on it was not that far down. That evening when I got home I called my wife but there was no answer I called her two maybe three times. She cannot be working because we usually worked together so she cannot be working late I began to hate her she was never at home.
I looked in the freezer and looking at the possibility that she may just be out, the theory had to be considered considering my situation the freezer was quite full. I put the food that I had chosen on the kitchen side. Then waited for it to defrost as it did I began to chop it in to small pieces. But as I was chopping it became more and more intense the chopping became harder and harder
and as it did the thrusts of the knife became more and more violent as the tears streamed into my eyes as I realised the things that I had done and the things that I had been doing.
I had visited the church two or three times this week just to make sure and see who was hanging around the area. It all seemed nice quiet to me. I was wearing a rain coat and in the pocket I had a small bottle of whisky. I opened the small bottle and took a mouthful gulping gently and waited for the numbing feeling.
To take a life that was the question what kind of person was I and furthermore what was I going to become. I took another swig from the bottle. Then I began to convince myself that I could get away with. I had to be good with myself to be able to question it. Something knew had occurred in my mind and behaviour I started to forget as I was thinking and it was so intense I slipped as I was walking lucky I braced myself as I hit the hard concrete floor. I laid there on the church floor deciding if I should get up I checked my self over nothing was broken or sprained. I sat upright gathering my thoughts there was not a mark on my body. I pushed my hand through my hair I walked slowly window where I could see my reflection with the darkness over me I

moved quickly into a more lighted area. I was focused. When I got home I walked to my study in there was a large book shelve and in the very middle of the floor was my chair. I looked at the chair I wanted to sit on it but the feeling was orc wards so I pushed the thought out of, it was a pleasure just having it the same room as me the chair was worth around a million or two any way that's irrelevant to the story. I shall continue. I leant forwards and stretching out reaching for a beer which was on the table in front of me. I closed my eyes knowing that if I was to sleep I would be bound to have a dream. I clenched the bottle more tightly as I passed in and out of consciousness until I feel a sleep. I was dreaming the first place I went to was outside then upstairs, then I was outside again but in this case I had actually walked outside and then I woke up outside. Being out side and being asleep did not do me any favours I was standing up right and the sweat was pouring off me it was extremely real in my mind. I could feel the power of the dream it was so real. When I finally awoke and had gathered my thoughts and mind I really wanted to find out why this was happening to me. In reality I was the only person who cared about me and that's all you need to know.

When I finally got back in doors I told myself over and over like I normally would it was just a dream and that the effects would slowly pass. A little while later I came around I found that I was completely covered with sweat I had to changed my clothes. I could not tell the wife mind you she was never a round anyway. I thought about going to my doctors just in case as the dream normally happens once a week but just recently it has occurred a little more frequently. I was not a great fan of dropping myself in trouble. I could see it now in big bright letters across the front pages of the hospital newspapers Doc dries up, or even so doc goes crazy, doc has crazy nightmares.

Or even worse crazy doc in psyche dream. I do not know they could write anything if I was found out but I was going to keep silent and hold my tongue.

It was around April my wife was coming home a little more often but she still did not speak to me.

I had to really push her to make a conversation with me. I hated it, I had not forgotten that I was going to murder her. The power of the thought could have reached her if she would listen to my mind.

Maybe she thinks I was having an affair. Everything was in a muddle, maybe she wanted a child. I did not think of that, but I just did not fancy her anymore. We were at the dining table I ask her to pass the

meat she did it then I asked her to pass the wine which was on the dining table she did that too. What was wrong with her or maybe it was me.
I looked straight at her I Looked into her eyes so sensitive and kind of beautiful, but I did not love her any more. In fact, the look on her face when she was eating was like a donkey. Mind you the food that she had cooked was good. I asked her who prepared the meal she replied takeaway there was a short pause in her breathe then she answered it yours came from the local takeaway. She put her head down and continued eating. Then she raised her fork and pushed out her chair, stood up and said quietly said that she had enough. She corrected her plate by pushing the knife and fork aside together. Then she walked out she said as she passed me that she was going to lay down.
And that she was sorry. She did not know yet but she did not have a chance. As I sat there the adrenaline ran through my body I wanted to run upstairs after her while I was thinking about killing her. Later that evening after dinner which I had alone I pushed my plate aside and touched my face on the napkin it had not occurred to me yet what I was actually trying to do and what was going on. I thought of contacting my brother he was a priest most of my family were wrapped up in religion but it never really meant anything to me. The thought of the day when I would murder my wife was slowly arising and for the last three months that is all I had be thinking about. I was going to say what I was going to say and that was that she was a real bitch. And if it was not for my studies I would not be going through this. I finished the glass of wine at the table then got down of the table. I called my wife down to me it was obvious that she would not answer I called out again but nothing but silence.
I went to the table picking up the empty plate and took it the kitchen I put what was left into the bin and dumped the plate in to my sink. That's when she called for help I did not know where in the house she was the calls continued the thought was to leave her stranded, I stayed in the kitchen and quietly closed the kitchen door still hesitating and waited for a real scream out again. Later on
I went to the fridge and grabbed myself a beer I quickly downed the beer and finally made a decision with great consideration for her I could throw her out of her home and with my own assurance I had found the perfect sound spot for her.
I presumed she was at work that's when the weirdest thought came into my mind that she was still in the building. I ignored the thought it

was just me being paranoid. I was thinking about her and I was thinking that she was having an affair which is a good excuse for murder. I checked my mobile phone for any messages, there was none. I went for a walk to clear the air.
As I gathered me belongs which was a ruck sack at the time I found a bottle of beer in the bottom of the bag I pulled the bottle out it was warm and shinning and light. It was a struggle to open it at first then I gave it a bit tug and it opened. I took a mouth full the taste hitting me hard then the soothing came. I took another swig and then another until I became light head. I wanted another one and I found another which I could not believe it. I was now half drunk and I was trying to figure out when I left them there.
I continued to think about her and when would the chance of her murder would arise. I had a couple of places where I could hide the body. The second place was in the church and lucky enough they were everywhere so I had a wide chose. The thought was to bury her on top of something that had already been buried. It could work.
I went to sit down on a park bench I felt so aggressive towards my wife I did not realise but I had clawed a chunk of wood of the bench. As I was drunk I and was lost as I must have walked and walked with the thought of the wife. I looked into the ruck sack for the map I could not figure it out one minute I was walking in right direction and then in another, it was now getting late and the sun was going down and it was going to get dark soon. I was lucky enough to find the mobile phone but not lucky enough for it to be charged. As I making the phone call to the taxi firm it ran out of power. I of cried. I had been in the area for a couple of hours and I was getting sick of it already. I was going out of my mind plotting and thinking. I needed to find out a way to murder that bitch it was like poison
That's when I realised what I had said I had solved it that was the answer. Mind you she was never at home so how would I do it. I stayed on the road to find my way home I was wearing a rain mac.
I found my way back to the church benches I was just about to give up through tiredness when a parade came walking past. It looked to be a holy parade they all had big flags and they were singing and dancing. I stood up and in a moment I had joined the long line of the parade just to see where I would end up I was hoping that they would march me back to town where the hospital was. But the parade did not and I was even more lost than I was lost I in the beginning. I stepped aside just on the curb took a deep breath and walked the opposite way. That gave

me the idea of that if I could get her walking into the country side I could do her murder there and I would be in a perfect place to hide the body. Even better I could leave at the side of the road and make it look like road kill. I decided that it would not work. The continued I could always push her out of the car and make it look like she fell out, that would not work either. What about a cycling accident that was a stupid idea we do not have any bike mind you I would have to make it look like an accident.

The sky was dark blue the sun had just set and now it was dark and I was still lost. It had begun to rain I was sure by now that I was not too far from home now. In fact, I was only a few minutes away

As I got closer to the house the rain poured down and I was sure that I was just about to be struck down by the lightening which came with the storm. I was glad I did not look up as I was that sure.

I had found my home I walk in taking of my wet jacket and leaving it on the door mat with my shoes. I was tired and just wanted to sleep I went straight to my room and got into the bed I could not be bothered to undress, When I woke up I was coughing and thinking of my alibi. I laid there semi-conscious and half asleep

Being in my bed was a luxury for me as I was a doctor I spent most of my time on my feet and I have fallen asleep on more than one occasion standing up. So I laid their wake enjoying the moment

As the evening became night as I laid their I jumped up in shock I was looking for my mobile phone for some reason I thought that I had an exam. I scrolled the Calder down looking desperately

Trying to find the exam date I found it and it was not until tomorrow. I did not need to revise as I was good enough to pass the exam myself, The next day I woke up nice and early, the exam was dead on ten o'clock.

By the time had got up and washed and ready I made my way to the college I cannot recall what it

Called I walked in just in time to receive my paper as I sat down and that's all I can remember. A s I awoke I got up crumpling the exam paper s into a bundle shoving the desk forward and the chair back. I could not believe it I had fallen asleep and missed the whole thing. I walked out in a slow sleepy way bumping into walls and tripping up once or twice. As I found my car I could see as I came out of the college. I looked at my watch ignoring what the time was and thinking how was I going to kill my wife and when was I going to commit it and the question was how was I going to get away with it. What I needed was an alibi I closed my eyes drifting in to my mind which was poisoned with the constant thoughts of murder at last I was going to find my true self.

I walked out in anger she could not even be bothered to say hello or good morning it was natural for me to understand my own behaviour as I was a doctor it was a bit out of her character. That's when I decided that I really wanted something to happen to her I had decided that I did not want her any more. She was too much to handle and on top of that I did not want anybody else to have her. So what was going to come of this.

My mind was racing I was at the exam table I was thinking normally again although I thought that the teacher at the exam was talking to me it was that intense all of a sudden for some strange reason not realising I stood up and not knowingly shouted out. I shouted out the word murder.

And sat back down only to quickly decided to gather my belonging in this case was a ruler, calculator and pen and left the exam room. I feel asleep in the corridor for an hour or two in fact I the other junior doctor s woke as the exam was over and I arose to the sound of a school bell on top of that.

I was getting focused on my day it was not getting any easier it was not a lot to put up with for a person who was my age I was only young I was about ten years younger than my wife. I was slowly getting drunk and this was what my day and this was going to consist for the rest of the day. As the day went on l managed to pass out twice once in the kitchen then again on the dining table. It was not particularly comfortable. I went to the lounge to sit down half hung over I slowly fell asleep,

I sat there just staring at the chairs counting them over and over one two three four five and again and again. The table was covered with a checked clothe and in the middle was a vase and some flowers, and a small pot of some kind of incense. I could smell it as I became more and more aware of my surrounding then suddenly I awoke it was as fast as that a few minutes later reality kicked in dam, dam I said then shouted I'm going to be late the exam when I looked up that's when I saw her she was just standing there with her arms crossed she pulled up a chair sitting down on it opposite me. You could off have woken me up. I jumped of the seat and ran out of the room in to the corridor grabbing my jacket slamming the door on the way out I was on my way to another exam late.

When I got back I tried the door handle slowly and quietly turning to the right it made a large clicking sound and opened it. I could not believe it I was in at last. I closed my eyes for a second with relief.
It was four forty-five in the morning I had another exam at 7 o'clock there was no point in going back to sleep I walked through the hall way there was a kind of sombre feeling with me and I knew that it was me and only my wife that could sense it.
Going all the way back to the cold that I had it had become a sniffle I would sniff occasionally.

It was not like me but I had to have drink I found a bottle of beer in the kitchen and opened it quickly and drunk it even faster. The sky was light and lit up brightly you could still see the moon I always thought that the sky was one of the most beautiful things that had been created. Looking at it filled my eyes and made me wonder what was out there. Sometimes I would just stare and gaze it was rather hypnotic. I could not recall where many of the conciliations were and I only knew the names of a few. It seemed to me to be great knowledge in its own beauty
I did not want to admit it but I was so board of her she would come home she would clean, cook and study no sex that was it. I had got board of her. Maybe it looked false what I was going through I do not know. We would sit down together and she would not say a word these long periods of silence were getting annoying and her tiring behaviour who could understand her I certainly could not. I was not thinking about myself but I think that she was sick as sick as me. I was sick of her silence and I was sick of being with her although there was nobody else.

I clumsily walked back to the house towards the back door and used all of my strength to try and open it and force my way in. I had my watch on I checked the time 4.00 o'clock on the dot. I had to get back in side as I had an exam in the afternoon. I tried to jump up on to one of the walls I was too short and to skinny to pull myself up to a window the walls were stony and there was nothing to at the bottom of the wall to help me up. After making myself look like an idiot I walked casually to the garage to see if there was a ladder I was confident that I was going to find one. I opened the garage door slowly. In side I could see that my car was still there while I was looking for the ladder I was thinking about my wife and how I manage to pull her, I said to myself quietly she's a doctor and then I said I'm a junior doctor I continued she is my wife. And she six foot tall and I'm five two. When we were together she used to call me shorty. I would always take her jokes not that she was particularly funny anymore.

As I continued to hunt for the ladder I stupidly bumped into an old car battery it fell off the side and landed right on my foot. I limped around the garden in pain it was a large garden with trees and a few bushes knowing that did not make me feel any better. What made the injury even worse was that there was concrete patio just before the garden and then a pebble floor this did not help my situation I know had limped across the garden and fell to the grass floor in pain. I could feel my body it was hot it was obvious that I was burning up I had a temperature and then cold sweats straight after the pain receded. When all the pain had gone I tried again this time forgetting about the ladder I slowly climbed the wall. As I climbed the wall I clearly see the roof of the house and near the top there was a window, it was open. As I was getting to top the thought of welding my keys for the back door was just sinking in, I had left them in my jacket pocket from the sleep walk. As the thought of knowing where my keys where I lost my concentration I slipped a little then a little more until I lost all grip and fell off the wall completely. I hit the floor quite hard but as I landed on both feet I did not hurt too much. Again I limped around in pain for a few minutes. I had given up I leant against the back door for a minute sucking the darkness into my mind the only thought now was to break in.

CHAPTER 4
Deeply in the darkness

I looked deeply in to the darkness it was a little bit exciting thinking that there was something there when there was not. As I was stuck outside I began to think about my condition thinking about what pill I would try next to cool myself. More importantly I thought of the tablet caused me to remember where the door keys were weird I thought for a second then bending down and looking under the back door mat

there sitting on the wet ground was the key. I smiled as I let myself into my home.
We both left the table my wife was not acting as my wife she was not being like herself. Whatever was in her mouth was just about to be spat out onto her dinner plate. I looked at the time it was eight o'clock as I did she asked me the time, there was a short silence then she asked again "what's the time ". I replied calmly eight O'clock. But I was not calm the rage in me wanted to explode there was nothing that I could hold on to I could have eaten the edges of my dinner plate. I could feel the sweat accumulating on my brow and slowly dripping down my face I was hot I could feel it I picked up a glass and looked into it hoping that I had not turned red. By this time, we had already taken our down into the sink then she spoke "so have you had a nice day". She asked turning her back on me.
I was dumb struck by this I actually had nothing to say at this time and struggled to spit the word's out then it happened uncontrollably "you bitch".
She replied with a what then I spoke again I said yes very good. She shunted to the left and slowly put the rest of the plates and cutlery into the sink. At this point I did not feel too good I had a spoon and again I looked at my reflection in it I was bright red. This time I chose to ignore this. As she turned from the sink she spoke to me again "How are your studies". The thought occurred to me that she was acting funny that's it I was sure or she was having an affair. It was plausible she was never around at night, the strong silences and every time I'm in the room with her she turns her back more so when we speak. Either that or she just could not look at me. I had to think that's what I told her I needed the space she just looked at me with agreement. It was all to sus pious. After that extremely small conversation and finished the washing up we went upstairs. When I got to the top of the stairs my wife asked me if I was okay I clearly was not however I was not in the mood for an argument either and I was too afraid to tell her. She went to the bathroom leaving to toilet door open. As I walked into the bedroom closing the door behind me. I slipped of my shirt and folded it dropping it on her dressing table seat, Then I removed my trousers and placed them on top of the shirt on the dressing table chair.
She walked in. "what's with the strong silence".
"It did not occur to me "I said back to her.
My reply to the rest of her conversation was that I was too tired and wanted to go to sleep.

I got into the bed the sheets were warm, I pulled the bed cover over myself it was warm. My wife got in also pulling the cover up over us both. I did not want to lead her on I just snuggled up to her but I could not take it just the thought of touching her made me swear. I leant over to the other side of the bed giving her the cold shoulder, she was fast asleep and I do not think she noticed. This did not surprise me I know was just about to close my eyes when I spoke out "darling what are you doing tomorrow". There was nothing not a word my wife had fallen asleep. So that I was facing her I turned on to my other side she was so beautiful but I hated her she did not move a muscle only that my approach had got her talking in her sleep. But that did not matter I looked at her throat her arms were kind of up from her sides and close to her face she was dressed appropriately I raised her arms of her face gently and touched her face. I touched her skin it was soft and white, I pushed her hair aside she was truly a beautiful woman that had to die. I paused myself for a second then putting my hands around her neck but not squeezing, she grunted in her sleep although she was not a whore neither was she conscious I put my hands on to her neck again softly and looked at her eyes and cheeks I began to squeeze just enough to wake her up. And just as I predicted she woke up and was awake I climbed off her as she clasped for air. I laid their next to her pretending to be asleep. She sat up half awake reaching for a glass of water which was on her bedside table. She then budged me but I did not move I kept my cool I did not budge. It was later that night when I was asleep when a large crash was heard. I presumed that the big, big tree in the garden had finally fallen down. I thought of getting out of bed but my body was not having any of it. After a moment or two the lights of touches and the loud voices of my neighbours could be heard. But I was wrong I laid there still half asleep, then silence I thought that I was dreaming as the lights and voices settled. My eyes half open I had to make a decision get up and go and investigate or wait until the morning. I decided to go and have a look around this time I was awake. As I got up I knocked my ash tray off the table on to the floor with an empty glass which was previously filled with beer. I was sober enough to go outside as I went on my way I was looking at the time three O'clock. I took off my pyjamas and slipped a pair of jeans on. When I got to the bottom of the garden there seemed to be a large creator. That's when I woke up. I picked up a t-shirt and put it over my vest, it was white and dirty this was also a dream. It took me around five minutes to realise this. I went to the bedroom window pushing the blinds apart. It was dark still and quiet, it was a dream also I took off my jeans and t-shirt and put my pyjamas back on. I sat on the bed in a most uncomfortable position everything we had brought for the mansion was mostly second hand I think that the only things that were actually new was our cars. The same thing happened the next night It was late I was lying in bed when again I heard a large crash which had awoken me. It was a strange feeling this time at first. The drool marks that had plastered one side of my face, the medication had kicked in. going back to the large sound that I heard I convinced that It was just a dream as I had the same dream the night before. I fell back to sleep thinking that I was alright I was a doctor by trade, I was constantly studying and it was the weekend's my days off in the evening's was horrible. I did not notice it at first but I was sweating. I got out of bed but within an hour I was back in bed. I was perspiring which I found quite hard to believe. I had become hot. I got up and went to bathroom. I had all the equipment plasters, stethoscope, bandages, antiseptic creams, sore throat sweets, paracetamols, and most important of all deep heat spay. By the time I had been through everything I had forgot what I actually forgot what I went to the med cabinet for then it came back to me as I noticed the sweating my body when I looked down on it was soaked. I was left in the cupboard knocking things over and down.

The bright lights that appeared had disappeared and there was nothing not a sound, no lights and nothing.

As I checked my self over my clothes were soaked not just the arm pits on both arms but my crotch as well. I stripped naked putting what I had on in to a linen bin. Just after I had done this I sneezed not once but several times each time holding my breath as I was smoking and slowly puffing what was left of the smoke out afterwards. I was lucky that I did not choke although there was a little cough afterwards. I hocked what was left in my nose into my mouth and spat it out into the toilet shutting the lid afterwards and flushing it away. I did not realise at that point that my mucus was yellow I always thought it should be green. Weird I thought as continued to the kitchen I had not eaten for a couple of days. I went down stairs to my pantry, but nothing it was empty. I was not particularly hungry although the thought of eating would have eased the pain.

I walked back upstairs to my bedroom and moved towards the window and sat on the day chair which we called the calm chair and spread my arms out watching the early morning arising from the edge of the window.

I slept through to the next day in the morning everything was normal she had not mentioned what had happened to her in the night so I presumed she thought it was a dream. There was more silent as we dressed she dressed me first trousers, shirt, tie and socks. Then she dressed her self-asking one thing of me which was to do up her dress not that she could have zipped herself up herself. She asked me where I was for the day I said I was not sure, then I asked her for her dairy she looked around the bedroom going through a couple of draws until she found it, and handed it to me You're in London she kindly replied that I would not be back tonight. I sat on my bed waiting for her to hand me my shoes. That's when I slipped up I stupidly asked her how did you sleep she turned around doing up her blouse. Saying fine you know crazy dreams about death and things my head nearly fell off. I bowed my head she noticed yes bloody dreams she went on. I interrupted dreams of what I asked slowly trying to find a way of changing the subject and avoiding the whole subject and conversation. She continued am I crazy or did you have me around the throat last night. I thought she had caught on but I kept my cool.
No, No I was by your side I said,
She replied with then what are these marks on my neck then. I replied what marks and pretended to look. There were some marks on her neck and it was obvious that she was upset I continued in saying something stupid a teenager could have made a better excuse well you're a doctor I replied so are you she said shouting and left the room. I sat on the bed thinking that it was over and thank god that she never took it any further. I could not stop thinking about what she said I closed my eyes and tried to change the subject that I was thinking about. I did finally after a few hours but it was the expression on her face that I had a problem with. She walked out I followed her slowly closing the doors behind me. I felt sad as I put my hands towards my head, pushing my hair backwards. I could feel another cold coming on the air in the room was changing and the early morning dew was just unsettling as the sun slowly moved through the clouds of the doomed sky line.

I could not explain it enough to myself that I wanted her dead as I thought about it I thought that I thought about it too much I wanted her dead. How I was going to do it was a whole different matter, although the thought was overwhelming. The thought of the constant thought of the matter would not let me think about anything else. It echoed through my mind, I was thinking about the things she would let me do for instants she would let me watch her dress while I laid there on the bed. The hate for her. She was testing my eyes they were filled, what was I to do. I had one option I could kill her as I planned or I could leave her either way in wanted her dead, I wanted her hurt. I got of the bed. And walked into the bathroom and started to undress I was getting a shower the water was cool to my face and the sound of the water dripping made it even more tranquil, the touch of the water running down my back and on my shoulders was soothing I did not want to get out. After about an hour I got out. And grabbed a towel off the towel rail which was in front of me as I got out of the shower. Once I was dry I put the towel down. I got back into the shower to shower again as I did I came out with a month of abuse I was screaming and shouting to the point that I was punching the air the tears filled my eyes until I realised what I was doing. When I got out and got dry and went to my wardrobe to find some clean clothes. Once I was dressed I found myself a cigarette once I had finished it I put the cigarette out in my ashtray. I was not bothered about smoking but I was sure that it pissed my wife off and that gave me an excuse to do it and that was good I thought. As I moved away from the window putting the cigarette out closing the window behind me. The sun was slowly rising and the clouds were gathering around it, in fact it was a becoming a bit over cast. Then at a second glance it looked it looked like it was going to rain. I wanted to go outside but there was storm that was coming although it seemed to hold back. I always had a passion for the rain I believed it was one of our greatest elements. I quickly grabbed my hood top and stood outside it was a nice top and expensive, and it fitted un like most of my clothes. I pulled the hood up and walked outside.

The storm had started the rain poured heavenly down upon myself as I watched. It was cleansing with the weather at this moment came thoughts as I took my mind off the rain I thought of god. I closed my eyes and once more thanked god. When I got back inside I walked to the kitchen. I was pretty drenched and soaked through I made myself a cup of tea and soon afterwards decided that I would hit the bottle I finished the cup of tea and grabbed my bottle of beer. The taste was good, my wife was not in and it gave me a chance to think about her murder. It was always easier under the influence of something, I continued to plot and plan how was I going to do it. I sat down on the chair in my study my head in my hand's what a gift I thought I needed to find the answer, and I needed an alibi I had watched all the programs on TV. It was not that I just wanted to murder her it was the fact that she was driving crazy. The only thought for that moment was that I would be better off murdering her in her bed while she was asleep. But I came to the conclusion that she would be sleeping lightly after the previous night and she would be sleeping lightly. And I had the worry that she would wake up while I committed the deed. Then I thought I could wait until she was ready for work I could make an attempt in the morning but I figured that it would be too early and somebody would hear but we had close neighbours. I looked down at the cigarette it was slowly burning out I gave it a quick puff and got it going again I thought how I was going to finish her off I needed to take it step by step. I went to my bed I needed to sleep. I got into the bed grabbing the duvet pulling it up over my body up to my face and eventually over my head. I continued to myself that it was not my fault even though it had not happened yet the murder that is. I was sure that I was being tested and I had been tested before I was not one for games and this one was a big one. I had awoken I got fresh which was a wash my face looked haggard what had happened, I touched my hair and it was falling out I in an instants blamed her for it. I picked up a cigarette and lit it up my hand s were shaken. The smoke soothed my mind and the good feeling of inhaling the smoke into my throat. When I looked back the loss of hair looked good it kind of gave me a new appearance. I was not particularly noisy but there were people walking past my house. My wife walked in she was bright, tall and good looking I had not the time to tell you everything about her but she was a bombshell in my eyes, except she had a big mouth its funny you know their always something women they are never perfect. She was like a crocodile with her gob snapping at everything it just did not suit her looks. It was like falling into a fantasy, everything about everything then nothing. When we first met she spoke about anything about anything talk, talk, talk.

The winter went fast it was late in the summer time when we got the invitation to a wedding it was my nephews wedding he was only thirty which was good and his wife was around that age too as he was so young I just hoped that he would or could hold it down. We both were delighted and we looked like it although I was thinking that my wife was over acting a little bit. I think she was putting it on, well I thought so. In the end we had a great discussion on the subject and in the end I decided that we should not go even though that I was delighted with the offer I knew if I denied her she would be upset. She was a little bit upset I comforted her for a minute but she got more upset then she got even more upset this was not like her. In a way I thought it was good a last she was getting a taste of her own medicine.

She was over acting I was sure she was putting it on well I was not convinced mind you she was in need of some comfort. Then I realised that she was in need of something as she was actually upset. I knew where this was going, it was going to the bedroom it was so obvious I should have seen it coming.

She walked off to the bedroom as I predicted however when I questioned her she explained that she did not want sex this evening, I could not believe it. I do not know why she said that it was not like I ever spoke about it we would just do it was never talked about. She was hesitant and she looked weak and frail she was in a good position to be dog meat and murdered. We continued the conversation about the wedding again and again I said that I would not go. I had to be hard as I was the man of the house, eventually she agreed. I sat down in the study and I thought that she was getting the better of me the more I thought about it the darker my thought's became and the darker the game became. I closed my eyes while I was on my desk when I finally awoke I could feel something but I was not sure exactly what it was, was not right it was like I was floating. I felt light headed and dreamy which was not like myself for the first time in a month I called my dogs. The

y were good beasts and it was my wife that usually took them for walks but in this occasion I would take them out. I wanted to invite the wife it could give me the opportunity to murder her. But then the dogs would be a witness so I guess it would not work. I called out to my wife where are the dogs there was no answer at first then I heard her voice out in the kennels. She was ready to take the dogs out I wanted to join her. As I put on a brave face as

I approached her when we came together I greeted her again kissing her on her right cheek, she was impressed and we wondered into the forest. The dogs were play full and I was enjoying the atmosphere until we were split up due to the dogs splitting apart while in play. I shouted out again and again but nothing, then I waited for a minute and shouted again and again nothing. It was bazar I took a cigarette out of my jacket pocket thinking and hoping the worst. The wind blew through the tree's it was like a dream it was like something a lost child would experience I could hear my consciousness as I remembered, all it would tell me at the time was to go. But go I wondered if the thought was that I should leave the wood I chose to stay. I stayed in the forest for an hour looking for her. Then suddenly she turned up out of the blue with both dogs. I was disappointed I bowed my head then looked up with a disgruntled smile on my face. Her answer to that was why was I looking that way, the look continued for another moment I struggled to change the expression as we walked home.

I sat down in my study griping a bottle of beer my thoughts for the day where getting better except they were just as dark it seemed to me the more I thought the darker they became. I was trying to understand them it seemed impossible they were so strong if you could understand the mind.

Any way enough about the dogs and there journey I had my own life to think about I want to go all the way back to the dream that I was having. The one when I was walking in the garden. Well I know that it was recurring what did I tell my wife as dreams that recur could only recur I did not tell anybody why well for one I did not have anybody to tell and two I did not want to because it was too personal. Although in this through this there was a man he was undressed and stood at the bottom of the garden naked anybody who was anyone would say it was a turn on but however it was not for me. I was trying to figure out what and who he was I had told my wife about this the man. I was sure that by now that she knew that I had been sleep walking, the number of times that I had left my wife bedside. The number of times that I had locked myself out outside the mansion in the garden. I closed my eyes nothing but darkness. I was kind of happy about that. But the man in the garden bugged me who was he. I looked closely at the man he did not resemble anyone that I knew he was an old school mate or anything like that he was not a relative as my father was dead as most of the family.

CHAPTER 5
SLEEP WALKING

Whatever
was going to happen I was half asleep and sleep walking as I moved slowly unaware down the stairs that I was paused at the top to begin with. The stairs were steep and orc ward and big and wooden.
The stairs looked old and warn but shinny in appearance, no carpet my mansion was large you could walk around it all day.
As I was walking I stubble down the stairs, as I did I feel against the window rather than the door in my case that was good. Although I was not outside yet as I went for the door. The only thing when I get to the end of the dream would be the cold wind which would wake me up then I would have to find the keys to let myself in.

I could see a hundred thought go through my head as she undressed I could see the undressed figure a million thoughts past through my head, what, why, when, how, as I slept. I was too asleep to really start thinking about it. I could see the undressed figure again a thousand thoughts ran through my mind. A s I thought I became more and more fatigued until I fell asleep. As I was asleep I kept the thought within me as I slept. I was not sure whether I was supposed to approach the naked figure, the naked man. I could see him from a distance in this dream I started to walk towards him but before that I was sleep walking out side. He seemed friendly enough, I asked him where his clothes were, he said in a weird voice he had none. The conversation ended as I turned around and walked towards the back door from which I appeared. I decided that I was awake enough to get him some clothes I looked for a t shirt and a pair of jeans and walked back out of the mansion to the garden where I had met him with the clothes. His stature was tall in height and his body warn and muscular.
But however when I got outside again the man had gone I went further down into the garden and called out to the man two or three times but nothing. The wind was blowing and the trees were taking it. I looked around the garden again and again until I was out of energy the mysterious man had gone. I placed the clothes down on the bench and took a step backwards then called out into the darkness as there was nothing there in reality so it seemed only the trees blowing in the wind and the echoes of the night.

When I got in doors and upstairs I was thinking about the man I could remember the man eyes they seemed powerful I sat on the end of my bed and closed my eye s I was thinking, thinking way back when I was a teenager even though I was just a young man as I was pretty successful on TV I had my own setbacks and as my mother was a doctor after being fired from the show I had decided to become a doctor. I had tried to use quite a bit of medicine to experiment. I had always thought that it was okay but I was wrong. I Thought that the decisions that I made as a teenager were right but in fact it was opposite the decisions I made as a teenager were wrong. As I found out so I decided to follow my mum it may sound sad but it is true. I used to take her pills just to see what the side effects were; my mum had loads she would not have noticed. As I came from a reasonable rich family her bathroom cabinet was full of all sorts of parasitical medicines, so I would pop a few tablets. I went to my wife's cabinet in the bathroom to see what she had in. I was quite surprised to find that there was a lot there must have been at least forty different types I guess that why she was flipping happy all of the time, and why my soul was lost. I picked up a couple of bottles and twisted the cap off the top. There was a mixture and they were all different colours, with their own individual and different flavours. I tried the first tablet it tasted vile I had to spit it out I could not take the taste. I did not even have to swallow it, I spat it out into the sink and quickly poured myself a drink of water as the taste dispersed I went to the next tablet and then the next what I was looking for was a sweet taste. I was beginning to think that my wife had not taste buds as all the medication, well they were all quite disgusting. I was not going to give up leaving the medicine cabinet tidy as I found it I went back to the bedroom. I sat down on the edge of the bed right on the side I was looking at the duvet it was grey as were the pillows although it meant nothing. I got undressed and removed my shirt and just laid there on the bed. Maybe I should just poison her, she had enough tablets to kill a couple of horses in there. A couple of days later I was in the garden in the early evening waiting for the mysterious naked man who had no name. All I could remember about of him was that he wore no clothes and had piercing blue eyes and his hair was a dark grey. He did not turn up at this point, I was going mad now it seemed to me that I may have been dreaming. It seemed real. I sat at the bottom of the garden for a couple of hours waiting but nothing.

Who was he

Any way I thought that whoever he was I had enough of his game I called out who are you, what do you want.
And it got me so angry I swore and shouted out rude words to god I was upset and angry as I said I was slowly losing my cool I sat down on the garden bench the feeling in my feet had left me as I stared into the darkness of the night hoping that I was not going crazy. The feeling subsided and I calmed down I walked slowly back to the house. I pushed the door open with a bit of force and slammed it shut behind. I walked into the living room and sat down on a chair just as I did the phone rang, but I was to slow to answer it and they hung up, all I wanted to do was to get drunk, and out of what I had experienced behind me it was not pleasant. I went to the fridge and took a beer out what I needed was a plan a really good plan when I went to the fridge I found a small tub similar to the small tub that I found upstairs in the bathroom cabinet. Just out of the corner of my eye. At first I did not think anything of it as I thought that the tub was some kind of medicine the name of it echoed through my thoughts I was trying to recall the name my conscious took me back. I poured myself a drink, I noticed my wife s cabinet out of the corner of my eye at first I did not think anything of it. I was tempted to pour myself another drink s I thought about it I noticed that the medical name on the medical box was not right it was completely different.
I looked inside of the pill tub I was not impressed, I did not know what my wife was actually into. She really took that many drugs, as I looked onwards and investigated there was a sliver tablet and lots of them. I thought that having so much medication around us could leave me at an advantage and that was good and the thought that came to my mind next was I could poison her. So the plot to kill my wife went on it had to be perfect plan every inch the plan now was to poison her at the dinner table it had to be perfect as soon as the deed was done and the police investigated there would be no clues. But it could not be just any dinner.
It had to be a dinner party that was to kill for so I invited a few of our friends who if I get the chance kill also. So that was the plan, now I had decided her fate as well as her snotty friends. The dreaded plan was nearly done; I finally was able to sleep those nights of sleepiness were over. I had found a way I slept sombrely for a day or two I was not disturbed for a day or two. I had no relocation for a day or two the time or the date. But however I was excited, so was my mind.

I awoke and with this I thought of the deadly deed which out a smile on my face a big smile. I could not work in fact I knew inside that this plan would work. When I finally awoke there was nobody around, I looked around for my diary which was always at hand I found it quickly and made the arrangements for the dinner party.
I waited for my wife to come home I was sitting in the place of the crime the dining room. She walked in about eleven o'clock in the evening I was half asleep in one of the dining room chairs my head hunched over as if I had hit the bottle and my arms supporting me. She greeted me as usual with a smile it was all false. Her smile was a little too sweet for me any how I replied with hello. I pushed the chair backwards stopping her from walking past me then I asked if she had a nice day.
She said reasonable.
Save anybody. I continued with a laugh.
She replied quite a few you know how it goes.
She knew I was picking a fight and before I had a chance to get started she continued that I was the big doctor that sits on his ass all day. She went on some of us have work that's WORK shall I spell it out for your lazy asshole a donkey works harder than you.
I attacked her back politely with look do not I am not looking for a fight, but I was. She stormed out of the room into another I called after her darling I continued and that's when I told her that I wanted to hold a dinner party. I said to her smoothly with a cool approach I know that we dine out most of the time but this will special.
Her reply to that was what was the occasion. I told her that she could invite some of her friends it would be good that we could get together. It would realise a lot pressure, I went into detail a lot it took me about two hours to convince her in the end I just walked out but however a few minutes later she walked in and agreed. She kissed me on the cheek of my face and said thank you.
I kissed her back passionately and thanked her I told her that she makes me really happy that was a lie. I could feel the expression on my face change, second the temperature in the room. I had a super tense feeling in my face. I wanted to throw up but she was standing right in front of me in the end I walked out ignoring her pleas to come back and finish the conversation by this time I had a mouth full of sick. I just made it to the bathroom and unleashed what I had in my mouth. I needed some fresh air at this point I did not know where the wife was. As I walked to the bottom of the garden the old man was

there sitting on my bench I tried to us him away but he did not move or say a word. I did not want to scare him and I certainly was not going to shout at him although I wanted to. It was like he was not there as I had not been too close to him I was a little reluctant to approach him as I was not sure that he was real. I pulled myself together and plucked up the courage to make an approach. I walked a little bit closer asking him who he was. There was no answer I continued what do you want there was no reply. I had to get back in the house before my wife would suspect something. I continued for just one more minute trying to get an answer from him but the more I
Persisted the further the image got until it disappeared that's when the wife came outside I quickly closed my eyes I stood there in the dark. She spoke out asking what I was doing and what I was doing.
Err just looking at the stars would you like to join me.
No she said then she shouted when are you going to grow up you're a bloody child grow up.
I could tell that she was in a bad mood. She slammed the back door as she walked in.
Good I was on my own again I stood there for an hour the old man did not reappear.
Who was this strange man one minute he was there the next minute he gone it was quite scary? The thought stayed with me as I sat down I was searching my mind for a reasonably good answer to the hallucination but I no answer. I was tired and had no act. It early morning as I got up out of the chair, I called out to the wife but there was no answer I could only imagine that she had gone to work. She had forgot to wake me again I knew that she left me sleeping on purpose. We used to go to work together.

I was caught into minds I could not turn the car around as I was on the motor way. So I did not have much of a chance. I kind of forgot about it as I pulled up to a restaurant that I was meeting her at. It was nice I have to admit. I walked in and saw her sitting there at the dining table. I had some parietal in my jacket pocket but not enough to spike her drink. The only other thought was of god and how he was going to have to stop me. I picked up the menu and pulled a packet of cigarettes out of my jacket pocket. That's when it occurred to me why I was meeting her here it was our anniversary. Luckily She was stuck behind the menu card. I leant back in the chair afar as I could go reaching out

towards the table besides me. Watching her and the opposite table reaching out for the flowers which stood up on it I grabbed them quickly just as she put the menu down. And approached her with happy anniversary daring handing her the flowers. I know I had a funny look at on my face. Then she spoke out was that supposed to be a joke I caught and shyly said no darling she lost her temper again and shouted you are a bloody waste of time then she stood still shouting. The restaurant went quiet for a moment then she continued like a spoilt child she was clearly upset. And then she stamped on the floor, throwing the menu at me and stormed out.
Was Err she crying I said to the waiter who picked up the menu. She said nothing. I shouted out I think the tears were a little bit over acting. I continued to shout she's a fake. I knew she was upset I apologised to the other guests for her outburst and went after her. She was outside wiping the tears off her face. I told her that I was sorry but it did not mean a thing, I was telling her that I had been under so much pressure at home and at work. I was making all of this up and I think that she was buying it but she was not she was quite on top of things she wiped the tears of her face with her hanky. She walked back to her car and got in as she was pulling away the window came down and she spoke out of the window and said that she hates me. Now I was tiring to stop her from leaving, I got into the car she threw me out I was standing in front of the car she reeved her up warning me I was in front of the car spreading myself across the bonnet and shouting she knocked me off with one more attempt and drove off. I was kind of happy that she had gone.

That afternoon I went to work I got there just in time I knew it was going to go wrong as we worked in the same department. It was late when I got home and even later when she returned.

What I had in my hand was her dairy it was the A to Z of everything it was filled with numbers and addresses. I did not know that she was as popular as that. I had totally forgot about the actual plan as I was thinking of it my wife walked in.
What s up.
I was too busy calculating to answer her.
Then she saw the dairy and snatched it back going into one okay I said smoothly I was in a daze.

I was trying to hide the look on myself just as she told me to change the way I was looking. I walked out of the room and quickly ran upstairs to the bathroom to take a look at myself. The walls were white and it still smelt of the sex we had on our wedding day. There was nothing wrong with the expression on my face as I was in the bathroom I turned on the taps and ran my hands through the hot water for a moment and then put some on my face. I was nice and cool again.
I was beginning to think that she also had a problem when I asked her she replied no. I believed her although I still wanted her dead. So I challenge the subject as we both pretending to be friendly with each other I started with whom was she inviting around for dinner. She replied that she had forgotten and asked if it had to be this week. I was about to have a mood swing. "Yes" I called out it does have to be this week. As we were in separate rooms as the conversation continued I had a smile on my face I called out to her again it's got to be sometime this week I rubbed my hand with excitement the sooner the better I called out. Her answer to that was could I pas her dairy. I could not find it she called out again it was on the table it was not there I called back then it is on the book shelve. I eventually found it. I opened it up like I said before that is was filled to the brim with contacts. I ran my finger down the long list of names. Later on that evening I was casually sitting in my drawing room with a hot drink which was now cold before I could find the answer to the question that I was thinking about the wife walked in. she went to greet me knocking the cold coffee over me. Which was a good I replied that was my pick me up it was a good job that it was cold. At that time, I believed that she had done this act on purpose and another fight began I said to her that she was lucky as it could have been hot. And I said a bit more after that she was not happy she threw her arms up in anger above herself. I stood up and laughed at her she ran out of the room. I stood in the study with cold tea as a reminder. And as my temper grew hotter shouted you bitch which was a bit out of character for me but I enjoyed it. later on that evening the fight continued we argued again I had got the upper hand and I was slowly getting better at these arguments. Eventually she bowed down to me she apologised and basically said the same as me she was having a stress full time at work. Then on top of that she said that she had been boozing I asked her if it was a lot she said no. we discussed this for hours the kind of places that you could end up and the people that you could meet. In the end

she said that that was enough and went to bed. I went down stairs forgetting that she was asleep I walked into the room speaking loudly to myself I was chanting it was going to be a beautiful day. Repeal as I opened the curtains wide knowing that I would awake my wife from her beauty sleep knowing that the bright light from the sky would wake her up and being woken up like that would put anybody in a bad mood. Hoping that the bright light would blind her awake. She did not move at first what a wonderful morning I said loudly, again she did not move. I got close to her close enough to whisper to her and I did I said something along the lines of I think you got the message I said those words to her standing right over her. She woke up after a few seconds. As she opened her eyes the words push off came sweetly out of her mouth. I told her that she was not that bad at driving I do not Know why I guess it was a conversation opener. She replied your pretty crap. She pulled the pillow back with the duvet back over herself and laid there for a moment s I was serving her some coffee. How did it figure I poured her coffee quickly had he thought of murder turned me into an intellectual even though I already was? Something had hanged and it was probably me. I began to think differently I had started to think like a killer I went outside to get some fresh air. It was extremely hardening on myself the thought gave me a rush I came over all hot. I had begun to sweat, my clothes were drenched and I could feel the sweat pouring of my head I had not committed the crime yet. My clothes were now dirty and I needed to change them. I had just changed them it was so hot and did not make too much different as I just expired any way again just as much. I looked in the mirror it was large and expensive and undressed slowly, first removing my tie then my shirt and so on until I was naked. I looked in the bedroom for something comfortable to wear. I unplugged the alarm clock listening to the atmosphere outside the wind blowing and watching the sky as I redressed, as I settled down I did not want to be woken. It Was around five pm that I finally awoke my eyes transfixed on my celling like the light in the room was too much and I felt light hit my eyes as I opened them. I was not myself it was a real struggle to move it was like my back was pinned to the duvet. I finally managed to get up it was like the whole world was on top of me I did not ever have a spinal I but It really felt hard that I could not move when I was down there on the bed. When I finally awoke I was feeling particular I climbed out of bed as it had become a struggle from now and adjusted the curtains so know body could see in, one of the symptoms of murder was darkness and I found it soothing. I was looking for my arm chair how could I miss it; it was right in front of me. I grabbed the arm chair and pulled it towards me and placed it in front of her. And sat down and watched her. I had left the arm chair before she awoke

I was walking down the stairs when the tears filled my eyes I did not know why I was crying why I was so emotional maybe it was all too much maybe I could not handle it. maybe as I thought for a

CHAPTER 6
TEARS

second that I should let her live. I closed my eyes and wiped the tears from my eyes I had brought from the boy which were in my shoe box. I sat on the side of my chair falling asleep sitting upright. Well I was kind of asleep it was more like a cat nap. The first thing I did when I awoke was to check the time. I know that when I got in it was fairly late the journey from the hotel which I will explain to you later was around half an hour as I drove quickly avoiding the police when I could. I clearly remember that the clock on the wall was twelve o'clock when I walked in.

She looked so beautiful just sitting there I did not move a muscle I did not dare move an inch. I was close enough to touch her hair but I wanted more I wanted to wait I thought of strangling her I was close enough and she was asleep enough. Although strangling her was not my style and that particular idea was too much or me to handle being so close to her was a turn on. Her blouse was partly undone. I could see her bra straps I thought about her for too long there was a bottle of wine and a wine glass close to her on the table by her side. She must have got drunk. I slowly reached out my hands stretching them forward towards her, I was just so temped to strangle her and get the murder done. She turned her head and raised her arm touching her nose she was on her way to waking up. I took a step back we were close to our fire place I thought of picking up the poker which was by the open fire place side. I wanted to commit her murder but in using a weapon there would be more complications and it was not my style. Besides what would I do with the murder weapon. Going all the way back this is how it happened. When I got back to the house all was quiet I put my keys in the door and slowly and quietly opened the front door I closed the front door quietly after me. I walked in neatly stamping my feet on the door mat, in a rush which was usual for me. I wondered where she was I called out but nothing. The boy's shoes were working wonders they were soft and feather lit I did not try and call out her name again and the shoes from the boy would make great evidence as they were not mine. It was perfect the shoes were not mine and through this it would help my alibi.

As I had left my shoes at the hotel there was no finger prints on them as I had used gloves every time I had put them on to wear, I had also lost my wallet I was cold and wet and exhausted all I wanted to was lie down on the bed after a hot shower I went to approach the desk clerk after great consideration I had no choice but to speak to him. I waited for a moment as I was walking in to the reception room I wiped my feet on the door mat. Making sure that I was heard just to get the right attention. With my head up I made my approach. I could not believe I was doing this I waited for the reception to notice me then I explained my situation, before he had a chance to speak to me I said something like this I had lost my wallet which true and I my car had broken down. And I needed a place to stay. I also told him that I knew my bank details I quickly recited them to him she took down my details and gave me the keys to my room. I took them quickly with a snatch we both thanked each other. I went up in to the hotel to find my room. Well I thought that was easy enough, I got upstairs into the room and put the kettle on then I turned on the shower and got into it the water was soothing, hot and there was soap. I rubbed the soap around my body making sure that I was totally clean and cleansed after I had finished I got out got dry and went and laid on the bed the room was large and it felt comfortable. Although it had a TV it was not particularly well decorated in fact it looked poor for the quality of the building. Behind the door there was a hotel dressing gown I put it on and opened the windows. When I looked outside I could see the police it made jump with excitement. It was all a little bit too close for comfort the next morning I left the hotel.

The now was to get back home I still did not know where I was and I was hoping that I was close to my home or my place of work. I now had to hitch a ride back to town I was on the side lane for an hour just as I was going to give up a car approached me it looked like it was going to stop but it did not it just drove past me. I stuck out my thumb again and again it was getting close to the afternoon. I could feel the weather changing there was a strong wind blowing and it looked like there was a storm coming. The wind was blowing through my hair as I looked around the sun was covered by fast moving clouds and I could hear the sound of the racing traffic amongst the sound of the country sides grasshoppers and birds hidden by the sound of the traffic.

With the rain now falling down I was not only without a ride home but I was getting wet and wetter by the minute It was getting colder the minute the coat that I was wearing was not particularly good in the weather my hands and feet were feeling the cold chill of the rain. My shoes were killing me like I was going to kill my wife. I thought about calling her to come and pick me up, but I could not begin to think that I was going to let her get one over me. I would rather walk in the rain on the hard shoulder on the motorway. I kept on signing the traffic as the rain slowly came to a standstill.

The road was wet and the number of cars that splashed me, well I had lost count. Finally, I was walking towards a junction. I could see a building it was a motorway hotel. That's when it struck me was I walking around in circles. I was lucky I was not and I had found another hotel. It was then that a man diving past me gave me a bit of road rage I did not know what his problem was maybe he was just having a laugh. However, he drove through a puddle and soaked I was not particularly bothered as I was already drenched from the rain storm. I did not need anything but a taxi as I was at the hotel I found one quite easily as the taxi driver was already waiting in the taxi parking bay. I jumped in and told him to take me to my home, but again I was taken for a fool as we drove around town and through untold number of roads I noticed that I did not notice any of the roads. It was clear to me at that point that he was taking me for a ride literary. I told the cab driver to pull over and got out the car I did not say anything he asked me to pay for the ride I pretended to look for my wallet then I thought I would just me straight with him I looked at him he looked back then I said it look I have no money I lost my wallet, look I said I will pay you double he began to turn red. Then he shouted name, address he handed me a piece of paper and a pen and told me to write my personal details down. I continued to walk on. It was not my fault I was convinced that that he was to blame He drove up beside me for a few minutes continuing to shout at me over the amount of fare that he believed that I owed him. In a moment he stopped shouting and drove by me stretching the car tires and driving off. I had to find out where was, I had an idea I had a map on my phone I started walking to find a road name. It was getting late I watched the sky for a moment I was just hoping that the power in my phone would last until

I found a place that I recognised I was worrying. I had no idea where I was I two choices I could walk back to the motor way hotel or I could keep on going I stopped for a moment to gather my thoughts. I decided that I would take a chance and walk it after a round of about forty minutes I found my way back to the motor way hotel. A least the maps on my phone was right.

It was extremely busy, people everywhere after a few hours I was set back into my working ways it did not take me to long to get into my job. I had totally forgot the time all I knew that it was the morning. I took my stethoscope off my shoulders placed it down on my table and sat down. On my desk was a computer and phone also on the table was a glass of water. In the draw was a small bottle of whisky. I took a glass and filled it half way up with water, and poured a small amount of the whisky in to it and took a big sip, I closed my eyes and fell asleep. When I awoke it seemed like hours in fact it was only few minutes, I went to find a waiting room to pass out in it. When I walked back in to emergency room it was packed people everywhere I had my stethoscope around my neck and I put on a brave face I got a good welcoming my presents practically stop the unit I was greeted with a few cheers and a hug. I got back to work. At the end of the day I walked back to my car I was standing over the bonnet thinking that I had got one over the wife I had a clean shirt in the back of the car on a hanger by the inside of the back door and noticed that I had a tie too. It was quite hard not to think of her now the more I thought of her murder the more I wanted to make it reality and controlling that thought was getting harder and harder. I was trying not to think about her. I had not been in AE for a month as I had been sitting exams I wanted to back in there but I was nervous and I thought of people questioning my behaviour sent the cold sweats straight back to me. I touched my forehead and gave it a wipe. I stood outside in the car park by my car getting changed. First the trousers and then shirt and tie. It was not particularly late and it only took me a few minutes to make the decision of walking back in there. As I had changed, all I had to do was to lock the car that's when I noticed the big starch down the door. I nearly cried my car my car I do not I was choking I continued verbally until the swear words came pouring out. I grabbed my bag off the floor and strolled into the hospital half crying and in a bad mood.

When I got there I took a deep breath and sat down in one of the patience chair for a minute or two. Then something out of the blue happened I saw my wife she was with a crowd of people properly other junior doctors I picked myself up out of the chair and hid amongst another group of people these were not doctors as she neared me I turned my back so she would not see me I was watching her she did not know she was big head I could hear her boasting as usual although I could not explain what she was saying. I wiped the sweat of my head.as I said she did not see me as she passed by. I followed her and her team to the coffee bar. She was in the cue for around five minutes I knew this was my chance to embarrass her as she paid for the coffee. As I approached her head down I on purposely bumped into her spilling her coffee over her I did not stop to help her or apologise I just kept my head down and kept walking. I did not wait around for a reaction. But when I found a safe place I had to laugh even though that was my very first practical joke. A s the night went on I was in a reasonable good mood and in my case was really good.in fact I could not stop laughing over the incident. I went on as lights on the ceiling began to seem to reach my conscious it was so bright in here you could wear sun glasses. I waited for her for ages I could not find her anywhere in the department I had to phone her to find out if she was still in but I waited until later as phone call straight away would too obvious and she would blame me which is what normally happens anyway. It was a good plan I went back to work I thought it was the best plan then I changed my mind

I went to the coffee bar by myself and brought myself a coffee just as I was going to take a mouth full I saw her. The coffee was hot and her appearance caused me some confusion and as it did I spilt the coffee not just over me but over any one that was beside and in front of me. That was it no more laughing that was painful. As I had lost her again as I was cleaning myself up she was probably in surgery frying somebody, so as I had some spare time I went to find her as I walked I past an old lady in a chair. She was slumped over and looked asleep. I was concerned so I tapped her on the shoulder but nothing I presumed that she had passed away. I checked her pulse again she had one that was good I was relived but I did not care. I tiled her head up she was grey and wrinkly and she had a pair of sun glasses on. I gently pulled them off her face and put them on. Cool I thought I thanked her for the gift and tapped her on her head, and said goodbye.

There was something wrong I knew as I could see clearly that my car had been smashed up it did not bother me although as it was already scratched across the door I did shout some swear words for a minute or two and it was possible that the person who scratched it up in the first place came back and did it again okay point taken I was thinking I totally agree. I continued the pursuit with a blistering conversation which ended with a dirty word.
I was on the way to another hospital I got to the hospital car park and found a safe place to park not that it made different my car was screwed and I probably would not make it home. I felt around the car passage seat for my stethoscope and walked to the main entrance it was reasonably quiet the long corridors and the smell of medication and old people.

CHAPTER 7
KEY RACK

It felt really good that I had my new keys for the car I had left them in the hall way on the key rack. I remember the key rack it was something that me and my dad made together when I was a teenager. It held sentimental values I was in my mansion with a really big smile on my face. I had not walked around the house in ages I was just running my hands across part of the lounge walls sucking in the memories. I went outside opening the large oak doors and shut the door behind me leaving the key in the right place so that I would find it if I went sleep walking. I went to the garage to look at the damage of the car I kept on saying it was a fucking porches'. Deep down inside I was torn up. She was a baby. I kind of mads myself smile I said to myself well it was still drivable but who was I kidding. I got into it and pushed the key in to the ignition it was not that bad I thought as I revved the engine I wanted to dive her I put the gear into reverse and slowly reversed out of the garage then back in it was not going anywhere. All I could think about now was the insurance, I was extremely tempted to drive her but I was sure that I would turn a few heads also now as it was late. I would probably end up nicked for turning a few people's heads. As I was in the bedroom now I moved across the room to its window which was open and closed it tightly. I got a little shock as I knew that I had not been in the bedroom to open the window and the wife bless her heart was not in, this gave me the suspicion that there may be someone else in the mansion. I closed my eyes and hope it was nothing. I had a quick look around but found nothing weird I thought. In the next couple of days my new car would arrive I was quite excited even though it was a company car as the other one was solidly mine own it was a porches and that was the beauty of it. I did not crash my car every day but I could not believe it when it happened again I was out driving the car on the same route when somebody tried to overtake me I did not notice at first all I know that it was a woman I did not recognise her. She was typically dressed head scarf and shades it reminded me of someone that I had scene before I had not been on the road for an hour before this rich chick tries to run me off the road. By the time I got back it was early morning the wife was nowhere to be scene she was probably on nights least I came back in one piece with the car. It was a quick decision to back to the hospital but I was not going there to get her I was going there to spy on her. Just before I went out again I got redressed I was in all black.

It was an extremely large mansion I cannot remember how large it actually was but off the top of my head it had may be ten maybe eighteen rooms I had not ventured into half of the rooms as in was always too busy I spent most of my time when I had it in the kitchen, study, and garden. The only reason that I would go to the kitchen was for a drink or maybe something to eat, the garden was about a fifty maybe a hundred meters it was extremely large there was a bench and a large lake which looked really beautiful in the winter. There were trees also surrounding the area it was my own personal space. The garden was well kept and the gardeners would come three times a year.
I looked up half drunk at my celling the echoes rang through my head like wedding bells stretching my mind back and forth I had a few more drinks I got up on to my feet stumbling across the room to find a window although there were a few I could not find one as I had not been this drunk months but just recently I had an excuse, a lot of things had gone on this year, giving up the TV show, medical exams, I was not a lazy doctor I told myself I also knew that my wife was trying to out class me. I thought one excuse was enough and that was enough.

I hunted around for a cigarette I had one in my packet. The mansion was filled with corridors it was massive it was worth around five million all in all. I looked up into the darkness looking hard at the sky and hard at god. The sky seemed friendly enough I was not sure what I was to think can you get an unfriendly sky. I walked further down the garden leaving the mansion doors open it was dark outside and darker in side. I headed back to the large oak doors. As I walked I was still looking up at the sky it came to my surprise that there were no stars just the dark worn out sky and clouds it dark inside and as I walked through the long hallways ignoring the light switches on the walls I found my way my study I found myself a glass and half a bottle of whisky. I opened the bottle and poured myself a glass in a tumbler and knocked it back after a minute or two the drink had set in. I walked to my armchair with the glass tumbler in one hand and the bottle in the other. I was thinking about the man who was he I began to think about where he came from people do not just appear and disappear it seemed that the man at the bottom of the garden was part of my imagination, it was well understood I thought. I was going through my symptom's and I was convinced that it was not a medical condition it just did not way up. For a while I was enjoying the illumination of the man because I did not think anything of it and when the man disappeared I was thinking at that time that it was real because it seemed to my mind that it was real. I had convinced myself over and over and told myself this was really happening. But in fact it was not happening after I had told myself that there had to be another solution to the vision. I gave my mind a really good check I stood up by the chair I could only come up with one theory I was cracking up. As I continued to drink new thoughts came and went I had begun to put the thoughts and feeling of her behind me they were not real just momentary I continued living in the past what was that all about all I wanted to do is forget, forget everything. But it was hard like her. I poured myself another drink. After an hour I was drunk. I sat there for hours enjoying the everything until I began to think about murder, and the stress of loving my wife. And the money that I would make out of her death the thought hit me like a thunder storm. I could see the expression on her face how could I forget. I think that I was thinking about it too much. I needed a break. I wanted to walk I knew a few places around the land. Although thinking about walking slowly took the other thoughts away but I did not push them away far. It was always like me to hide my feelings weather I was in a good mood or if I was in a bad one. In a way I had hidden part of my personality part of me. There was something inside me it was waiting to be unleashed.

I parked the porches up roughly part on the curb and part on the road. I did that because I thought it was cool, I got out of the car. I could sense something was a kind of dark sombre feeling came over my body it was the same kind of feeling that seemed to be at the mansion. As I was at the mansion I took my keys and opened the doors to let myself in as I did I turned off the alarms system by tapping in the code. I walked in the feeling was all over me. I took off my coat as I hung my coat up a flood of images filled my mind with thought on top off this I had a feeling that it all had to do with my wife the first thought was she was having an affair then the next thought was that she had killed herself. Or even worse. But what could be worse than that.

I was at work I all I wanted to do was go home hoping that I would not meet the wife and hoping that I had enough petrol in my car. I had changed my clothes I did not notice at that time that I had mud on my feet there was something new to me I had been doing things perfectly I had come a perfectionist everything I did had to be perfect I guess that is what come s with plotting a murder that I wanted. The perfect murder that was the only way everything that I did from that point was going to be perfect for example I had to change my clothes when I got into the car. And small things like the way I closed my curtains. In a way it might raise session towards myself but I was sure that it would presume the opposite. The wife had noticed this it was not hard to pick up on, in fact she had

Noticed she would ask me why was I washing cups and plates twice and why would I hoover the floor twice and other things she also noticed that I was now wearing gloves to do the washing up as before I was never bothered. It was like that; she was going nowhere good I thought that made me feel better. I closed my eyes and sat down after I had opened them I had a beer in my hand and opened it, it was well deserved. I was sitting by the window looking out into the darkness of the garden I thought that I saw something but there was nothing that was just paranoia. I began to think that it was only a few days to the dinner party and the murder of my wife I had decided that I was going to poison her. I continued to drink, I was completely drunk all the thoughts came plundering before me I coolly sparked up a cigarette what I thought who was calling the shots for me and how did he come to be. For once in my life I felt good and the pressure of everything was gone I could not answer the question that I was asking myself to answer. All I know is that I wanted her dead. She had played around with me enough; she had laid her final card. I went upstairs drunk and fell upon my bed the bed was nice and clean and there was a note on the bed, it said something like I loved the evening and she loved me. I read it again and again and again. I could not believe it I was getting a little bit upset was it a joke as I had been down stairs all day so who was the note for or from. I took another good look at it before ripping it up and putting it in the bin only to kick the bin over. I was quite sure that she did not love me, I took another sip of the beer which I was holding I was pacing across the room back and forth, the darkness felt nice for once it suited the mood that I was in. I closed my curtains and sat there in the chair in the dark. Nobody knew the kind of things that I was going through or the kind of feelings that I had nobody knew my problems I did not think that anybody really cared. It was something that I could not explain not just to myself but to other people

There was a disturbance and a disruption in my visions for the next twenty minutes I was really considering getting myself checked out but that would put a dampen the surprise I had for the wife. I did not even think about the risks that I was taking and I was sure that it was not just the drink talking. It was only after three or four pints that I began to feel better it was quite stressful being a murderer or should I say planning one. I could only feel guilty in my imagination as I had not committed the crime yet. Although it was just as bad as slavery or imprisonment just thinking about it which I was sure would come afterwards. As I recall you are not impression as such, most criminals seem to think that they maybe I was in at that point I had to ask myself was losing it.

I was looking deep inside my soul going deeper and deeper into my mind I closed my eyes. There were defiantly things going on moving images that I could see trapped my consciousness it was like I was being taken over. I would hear the odd voice here and there but it seemed to be getting more out of control as each day past. I had to question it I had to ask myself what was happening. I finished the beer and placed the can down on the floor I was reasonable happy after I had finished being a drunk everything had changed. I felt light and I wanted to fight which was usual. I was in a good mood I was skipping and jumping around the large rooms of the mansion and through the hallways. I had the music blasting out I ended up at my front door. With the music on I continued my way out side into garden I was feeling good but acting bad. I walked to the bottom of the garden, when I got there I was standing by my lake. I was so drunk I was trying to recite and shout out poetry. Pulling flowers out of the garden and pretending to be in love. This continued for about an hour. When I was done I sat down on my bench it seemed right at the time but I was very wrong I was not near sober and I was in the mood for a fight a verbal fight a verbal disagreement. Except there was only me the wife was not at home, it had begun I began to bottle everything up. I did not have anywhere or anyone to turn too I was too far away from my neighbours to approach them. I looked out towards the bottom of the garden it was a large garden as I had said before I enjoyed the view when I was drunk. My mind was racing and I could feel the expression on my change as my expression became more and more fierce, I could feel my face change. I was already at the bottom of garden when my mind was racing image after image through my mind it seemed like a life time but it was only a few second for a moment I thought I was dead, I had fallen into the lake it was deeper than I thought not that I wanted to be in there I was losing control for a moment I thought that I was going to drown the power of the vision was incredible when I climbed out on the bank I was out of questions I pulled myself further and further on to dry land as I turned over gasping for breath I saw the old man I opened my eyes wide I could not see or contain my feeling any more the feeling of darkness was around me again I was on my own the beer and the drink had nothing to do with it neither did the darkness, I wanted to change again and again but I could not. It was like a judgement. In the olden days if I was acting like I was It would be straight to the gallows except in my case there was no judge and no gallows there was just me. I was ready to put the last part of the plans to the murder together it was just a few days. I had got over the last couples of days and told myself to hang in there. The vision of the man I was seeing at the bottom of the garden on my bench had subsided, like I said in the beginning he was just part of somebody's imagination and I was not going to let it be mine. I never saw him again. As I moved from the thought of murder, the constant nagging and the pressure of my work was beginning to become too hard to maintain. All I wanted to do was sleep I wanted a fresh pillow in my face and a warm blanket, the pressure was on I could not just snap out of it I told myself I could do this it was not now going to be too hard in fact it was not exactly hard. I kept on giving my confidence the magic c I told myself continually to bear with it and hold on, just stick it out, and things like that. The thing that that impressed me the most was that I knew that I was sane and I was crazy so I was normal for a doctor to think this like this although the thoughts and the voices and the truths about being alive and being dead were a secret it was like a game you just had to get good at it and that's how we survive.

The time of the dinner party had come everybody that we invited excepted the invitation turned up, there were high spirits.

I thought this was my education you know the pressure of university and other things like family I think you know money and having to keep up with friends he's got it so I have to have it also keeping your self

I sat there in the cold looking room there was nobody around which was very rare I pulled out a packet of cigarettes and lit one up the smooth sensation hit my lungs and I was slowly awakening. There was always somebody who was smoking outside of the hospital most people just stood in the smoking area. Knowing that I was going to run out of cigarettes I made my way to the entrance of the hospital and waited and waited until I saw a young man I approached him just to talk to him knowing that he was smoking I knew if I could spend twenty second s with him he would offer me a ciggy and he did two in fact. I took the cigarettes and thanked him then walked off. Still outside I smoked the first one quickly the only half of the other. I was looking up at sky thinking that there was going to be another storm for some reason it always seemed to rain when I was outside but inside I knew it was me imagine I finished the smoke and went back inside. I was looking for the wife she was nowhere to be seen, which was usual for her as she was a work alcoholic it was funny that she spends all her time in this place I turn up and she disappears mind you that could be a good thing.

As I walked back in I went to the toilet to freshen up I did not think much of this I checked the toilet room to see if anybody else was in there. There was nobody in their only me these kind of places always reminded me of ghosts for some reason maybe it was because I was sitting on hell. As I had my spare clothes with me I had the chance to grab a wash and get changed I took my hooded top off and jeans and put a pair of trousers on.

l crept into the bedroom I knew where she was she was asleep I knew this you could call it intuition. If there was no music system then she was asleep in my chair, I moved quickly to the lounge to see her just sitting there in my arm chair. I could just make out the top of her head from behind her and her shirts sleeves. I kept

CHAPTER 8
CRIME AND COFFEE

my cool I had not committed a crime yet I sat down forgetting about the coffee I had in front of me. I was happy that the day was moving on quickly and it was soon to be night. Before I got into bed I could feel the pain it ran down my body into my toes that was from walking in under sized shoes and that reminded me that I would need another pair of shoes. I It took the thought and went to go to sleep. It was not good I was having a rough night tossing and turning all night long. I was a piece of shit if I did not get the right sleep in fact it made me feel poorly. I would normally wake up half way through the morning I will leave the rest to your imagination. In the morning I had awoke good as I slept good. I had slept reasonable well but woke up feeling half dead which was normal for me. It was an impossible feeling it was too hard to explain but it was not normal even though I said it was normal it was not. The first thing that I had to do was get some shoes from somewhere.

So I decided to get dressed all a part of the shoes which I had on and needed to find another, I went for a look around the hotel for another pair. I was looking in the changing room I kept my cool as I had not ever committed a crime before or that the point that I never got caught. I had forgotten about the coffee that I was thinking about I was happy but still upset that the day had gone and it was night. As I got into bed I could feel the cold making my feet cold I knew from that point that I was going to have a rough night. I could all ready feel the cold in my toes, I should have taken a more expensive room it was not like I did not have the money. As the night went on the coldness changed to pain as I had been walking I guess it was a reminder to find some shoes as I only had one. I took the thought to bed with me and thought about it until I had fallen asleep. In the morning I had awoke I had to get some shoes that was all that was on my mind at this time. I decided to get dressed with one shoe on and clothes of course I wondered around the hotel. I had not had a good night sleep as I woke up on the wrong side of the bed. There were shops in the hotel although none that sold shoes but as I persistent there was a young boy standing by a shop I looked at him I did not really want to approach him. I walked towards him taking a deep breath and calling him. He turned around hay I said what size are your shoes he replied what as first until I convinced him that I really needed them to buy I told him that I was in a hurry as I was a doctor on call, he just looked at me and then he said you want my shoes, how much I said there an eight. Good I said there perfect. I just said I'll give you fifty pounds for them but he said no I upped the price to seventy but he still declined. I asked him polity to come over to the reception desk. I asked the reception desk Clark to take out a hundred pounds out of my account then I gave her my details the boy had walked off I shouted after him look I've got a hundred pounds for you for them. He stopped and turned around He took them off quickly and passed them to me after I had approached him again. They were tight but they seemed to do. It was funny he took the money and walked off. Now all I had to do is find out where I was and get home. I checked out of the hotel and thanked the Clark and left. I had just enough money to get a cab home.

I decided to take my time in answering her I could clearly hear her as a dog's night what darling I whispered.
Are you okay.
This was great.
Darling. That's all I could say. Then there was a cough and the words of help me were echoing throughout the mansion. I shouted back hold on.
There was a long silent then a thud then I stopped and waited for a few seconds then I took the thud a little bit more seriously. I ran up the stair case lifting my legs up high like a fly taking two steps at a time. So far I had made it into the hallway. My wife was on the floor I was startled her hands were around her throat. I could not believe my luck. I waited for a minute enjoying what I was seeing, then I leant down over her and quietly spoke to her darling are you all right, knowing that she was not. I could clearly see that she had swallowed something. I wanted to do the medical thing you know pick her up, arms around the stomach and pull until the subject that was choking spat the object out. But before I was going to do that I was going to watch her suffer as I was. And I did, she was just about to give in, I could hear her heart it was so sweet boom bah boom. It was like music to my ears it was getting fainter and fainter, I waited until the last second before I applied the grip. For some reason I had let her live after everything I

had said about her and all the things that had gone through my mind. I knew the opportunity would arise again.

The time had come for the dinner party everybody that we had invited turned up. There were greetings and welcoming, with gifts of wine and flowers. We all sat down at the dining table in the dining room. Everybody was talking, it was incredible in could feel the hate, I was busy telling the guests that my wife was loving but a little big headed being a doctor of medicine. We were all discussing and boasting about operations and how many that I had completed. It went on and on. I was drinking in fact I was drunk. The thoughts echoed through my mind I was trying to stay sane as I served the first course. Around forty minutes later they had finished the starter. I asked if everybody had finished they agreed, I took the plates up and readied myself to bring out the main course. I had the poison in my pocket, I was keeping it warm, before I took out the main course I offered my guests some more wine and cigarettes. My guests were all drunk we must have consumed at least six bottles of wine and that was without the main course being served.
The tears began to fill my eyes this always happens to me when I drink too much, in my case it was normal. Although at this time I was trying to act sane at the same time. It was easy my emotions were getting the better of me on this occasion after a few minutes of crying my tears half running down my face I began to smile and from the smile turned to laughter. I laughed for a few minutes before entering the party again. I was pretty drunk and the music that was playing was stirring my emotion again. I took another beer from the kitchen side board and opened it I knew that I could not drink if I wanted the plan to work but somehow I managed to get myself plastered. It came to the point that everybody had eaten what was on their plates I cleared the table plate by plate. I was in the kitchen I could hear loud cheers and more laughter. I needed to be quick, watching the door way over my shoulder quickly sprinkled the poison which was some extremely strong mixture of tablets from the wife's medicine cabinet into what I thought was her next meal. Just as I did one of my guests walked in, I was already drunk and I was lucky that he was too, he went to take one of the plates I just stopped him in time. I asked him if he could wait and showed him the way back to the dining room. I did not think that he suspected anything at this point I did not know that I had mixed up the plates I was too drunk and I had to make a guess of which plate

had the poison in. I took the plates in two by two thinking that I should have poisoned all of them and that would be the last of them all of them. I should have been so lucky, I was getting excited as I watched my guests eating then suddenly out of the blue she asked me why was I not eating I said nothing I was hesitant I did not want to try the food she took another mouth full and another she looked up again. I slowly picked up my fork and took a mouthful again and again but little did I not know that it was my plate which was the plate which was poisoned I had poisoned myself to death.

www.ingramcontent.com/pod-product-compliance
Lightning Source LLC
LaVergne TN
LVHW090128160826
845673LV00015B/1112

* 9 7 8 1 7 8 6 9 7 9 7 4 2 *